WHEN WE WERE *Young*

Only Doing What They Understood

Savannah Kennedy

WHEN WE WERE YOUNG

ONLY DOING WHAT THEY UNDERSTOOD

The names of certain persons mentioned in this book have been changed in order to protect the privacy of the individuals involved. Some characters and events in this book are fictitious.

Print ISBN: ISBN 978-1-737-458-60-9

Digital ISBN 978-1-737-458-61-6

Book Cover Designer TMD Creatives, LLC

Readers 'response

Kennedy's relentless truths are captured and seen through the stories and insights of a young maturing teen, who is learning to grow, become culturally aware of herself and survive at the same time. It is in the midst of a 60's throwback backdrop. The book addresses the generational trauma of unlearned habits we "mindlessly" pass on to our children. It is a timeless reminder that life is a tapestry, connected by countless invisible threads. Each experience is woven into the "emotional well" we drink from and who we become...........**-Nyomi Simone**

Each character is a diamond in the rough going through a "process". We take wisdom from each other's journeys ....**-CJ Miles**

Sipping tea with an old friend and sharing "back in the day" scenarios......**Ebony Raye**

A village breakthrough.....when we know better we do better!.........**-Harper Collins**

TABLE OF CONTENTS

Dedication

Ralph Grant – My Dear Husband

Thank you for the many days you went out to work in the harsh cold weather and the sweltering heat, just to make this book possible.

You are appreciated.

Introduction

I was born in 1951 and times were quite different than they are today. Notice, I didn't say better but different. It was a time when African Americans were considered second-class citizens and Caucasians didn't mind keeping us in what they considered to be "our place." In New York City, the Jim Crow attitude of White America was very subliminal. Therefore, until it affected you personally, most times it was ignored by both parties. My parents were not front-line civil rights participants, but they still felt the injustices of the times. Having just won the difficult battle of escaping the south, they came to New York for a new life, new liberties, and new opportunities. They arrived in New York around 1952 which was a time when the spiritual mentality of oppression kept some Black people in invisible chains and caused them more damage than even physical segregation.

The civil rights movement started when I was quite young and while most people might find it odd, a lot of my early civil rights teachings came from the Motown music my friends and I listened to. James Brown was the first person I had heard use the term Black instead of Negro. Through their songs, Curtis Mayfield as well as the Impressions told the Black woman they were proud of her. Wow, Black men were telling the world they were proud of us. Motown also showed us three young Black women from the housing projects of Detroit, could gain worldwide recognition and become superstars.

But the flip side of growing up during this era was that society viewed long hair and light-skinned African Americans as superior. During that time, Black and White people alike found light skin and long hair more palatable and acceptable; and unfortunately, anyone darker than a brown paper bag longed for the advantages of their counterparts.

African Americans were not the only group of people trying to break free from under the heavy foot of America's inequality. Women in the 50s and 60s were thought to be nothing if they didn't have a husband. Recently, I saw a throwback satirical commercial from the 1950s. A woman asks a salesman a few complicated questions about the inner workings of a car she and her husband were thinking about buying. The salesman becomes frustrated with the woman's questions and resorts to what he understands. He shows his disapproval by asking her with quite a bit of authority "Where is your husband?!" in an attempt to shut her up once and for all.

Women are connectors and creators. They are the backbone of a family. They have been in time past and will continue to be in the future. I heard a joke quite some time ago that still makes me smile. I don't remember who told the joke, but here it goes, "A woman and her husband, who was Mayor of the city, went to a gas station. An attendant came out to pump gas and he happened to be an old high school friend of the wife. After leaving the gas station the husband said to his wife very boastfully, "I know you are happy you married me instead of that gas attendant." The wife turned to her husband and very calmly said, "If I had married him, he would have been mayor too."

I have managed to see the humor in my experiences and in the lives of all the women I have known during this era. I hope that in the pages of this book, I make you laugh out loud.

Hair

Hair is a woman's crown and glory. This revelation is realized early in a woman's life. As a young girl, a head full of long hair gives you the sense you have a bit of an advantage over the world. Later in life, this same feeling develops into a strong self-esteem. It is a woman's God-given right to flip her hair and bring a man to his knees.

The hair flip can denote a change in a woman's mind. Therefore, the atmosphere can shift from love to hate in a New York minute. Body language has the great ability to communicate more honestly than words. Hair-flipping has always been a powerful body language technique that women use to express their superiority over a person or a situation. Unfortunately, for some Black women, a lack of long hair has made this God-given gift belong mainly to White women. A young Black woman learns early in life her natural hair will never flip in the air with the mere toss of her neck. Her reaction to this eye-opener is a frustrated tooth sucking due to envy.

Straight, long hair seems to be the ultimate prize. No woman wants to feel second best to another woman. At one time, White women conveniently saw Black women as no competition when it came to sexuality or capturing a White man's attention. This long hair situation can cut to the very soul of a Black woman, so they had to figure out other methods to accomplish the same goal as the mighty hair flip. It always helped to have a strong flirtatious, seductive attitude without giving up anything. Working that big butt and bringing those swiveling hips on like a locomotive usually got a man's attention. Girls know it requires a strong sexual invitation to get boys to drop that precious ball and playhouse. That's why the subject of Black hair can be as explosive as a Glock in an inexperienced hand. I've seen a debate about Black hair turn into a nasty argument and spiral into a physical fistfight that easily separated close friends. A casual comment about someone's hair could get you cussed out royally or get your behind kicked.

To inherit what Black people call good Black hair is the luck of the draw. Long, soft, straight, or loose, curly, wavy textured hair is a recessive gene. So even with one parent having good hair your chances will always be one out of four to receive the golden prize. This Black hair business can play some very nasty tricks depending on who is in your family tree.

It can be devastating when your hair is so thin the strands of hair you do have will not cover your scalp. A bald baby is cute, but at the age of four and five the thrill is gone, and it is just downright embarrassing. There were quite a few horrible traits of Black hair back then. Those with a dead cotton texture that lacked life or shine no matter how much grease you put on it and some hair that just wouldn't grow. I guess it could have been a vitamin deficiency but back in the day the sophistication level to attack this problem with a biological option was not known. By the time you are eight, they have tried many store products. Then desperation drives them to Madam Uooboo mixtures such as sulfur, lard, castor oil, and even human spit. Believe me, the struggle has been real in the Black women's effort to achieve the elusive hair flipping ability. But whatever they concocted the hair would not grow or gain life. Lord give me and my mother strength.

Young Black girls with really short hair having just formed brief acquaintances with other girls will immediately tell "The Story." It has been a tradition over the years. I've heard the story many times with various twists but always with the same outcome. Now the story usually works best when you have someone to attest to this cock and bull story. The story basically goes like this, the girl in question with the very short hair tells us that in the distant past she had very long luxurious hair. But unfortunately, a terrible disease or mishap has befallen her hair and has brought it to the awful state you now see. But all is not lost because an aunt from the deep south would soon be here with some secret potion that would restore her hair to its original glory.

I personally, have never witnessed this amazing hair transformation take place. Because first of all, I knew it was BS from the start, and second, I knew it would take the Lord thy God to achieve this miracle and not somebody from a distant land with a can of magical hair pomade. To this very hour, these BS stories still continue to thrive because they are from the very depths of a Black woman's soul. Black women now have at their fingertips as much hair as money can buy compliments of our lovely Asian sister Miss Lee. The desire of the Black women to flip her hair and change the world can now be achieved for mere pennies. Won't He do it?

Over the years I have witnessed and been involved in different hair squabbles. Some I caused by my own stupidity and others were inflicted upon me. I had short, coarse hair that was super resistant to being groomed. My mother always braided my hair in small braids which I detested. They were short braids that joined together, and my mother had perfected this technique down to a science. Every part was done with such precision my head was now a human road map. These tiny braids made me look like Cecily from the Color Purple or the ideal slave hand. It was not a cute look. May the good Lord be with me.

When my mother didn't have time to make a million small conjoining braids, she made one large braid at the top of my head that swung to one side of my face. This braid always had a huge bow that matched my outfit of the day. To make matters worse, my grandmother worked at a hospital where she had what I considered the worst perk. My grandmother received the ribbons from dead flowers or from flowers that were left behind when a patient passed away. I actually wore dead people's ribbons on my head. This was truly a sad situation. Even at this young age I thought this perk was a stumbling block in my goal to look like a teenager. Since I had very little hair, my mother decided she would decorate my entire head with these awful ribbons and because they could be washed and reused indefinitely, they were the gift that kept on giving. In secret, I kept throwing these ribbons away every chance I got. But a hospital has an endless supply of dead patients and flowers, so I never came up with a plan that allowed me to get rid of all those horrible ribbons without being caught. If my mother had any idea, I was throwing away her lovely hair accessories it would have been my behind.

Being decorated like a kewpie doll was just another curse that came along with not having good hair.

Whenever my mother groomed my hair, she used a stiff brush and hard, thick grease to keep it under control for a good length of time. Therefore, my hair would require less of her attention. I was about seven years old, and it was the Saturday before Easter when my mother did something quite remarkable. She made fire come from a can. Until then, I had only seen fire on the stove. I thought my mother was a wonderful magician and she was going to do tricks for Easter. Well for witnessing this miracle there was a terrible price to be paid.

I knew my hair was going to be washed and done for Easter. So, I mentally prepared myself for the most dreadful time that usually occurred during the washing of my hair. The house was always in an uproar during this event due to my lack of cooperation. But I had no idea what a terrifying ordeal I was about to really encounter because up until this point I had virgin hair. This would be my first, but not my last nightmare with a hot comb. My mother had a comb I had never seen before. It was a big metal comb with a long metal cylinder. Around this cylinder was a metal spiral coil. It looked like a tool Dr. Frankenstein had in his hospital room.

My mother washed my hair, of course there was no detangling conditioner, so when she combed my hair out it almost killed me. There was nothing soft and manageable about my hair. It was a real tug of war that took quite a while to finish. The only saving grace for me was I wasn't tender headed. The problem was my hair was thick and very nappy. I now know how stressful it must have been for my mother to have one daughter with beautiful, long, easily managed hair and the other with a giant, steel wool, Brillo pad attached to her head.

When my mother had my hair combed out and somewhat dried, she would usually braid it and I would just go somewhere and lick my wounds. But not this time, it was Easter and she had other ideas. My hair was still damp when she put that hot fiery comb to my hair, and it produced a large puff of steam that went straight to my scalp. Back in the day, beauty shops were the only ones with blow dryers. I let out a blood-curdling scream; one that horror movie producers spend a lifetime trying to capture. Everyone in the house came running into the kitchen. The next-door neighbor even knocked on the wall. My mother told everyone "She's just being her usual crazy self and all of you know how she behaves whenever I touch her hair with a comb." But I was screaming, "Daddy! Mommy is burning me! Please, please make her stop." My grandmother said maybe don't straighten her hair this time. My mother told her furiously "Tomorrow is Easter Sunday, and her hair has to be done! I'm not going to be late screwing around trying to do her hair in the morning." My mother then turned her attention to me, "Go watch TV for an hour till your hair fully dries and you better know I will be straightening your hair today." My mother had no real expertise doing "black" hair and even less when it came to difficult black hair. She was never taught how to slay resistant black hair and transform it into white America's standards. She was only trying to make my hair behave so if there was a chance in Kalamazoo that I could actually swing my hair she wanted me to have a shot at it. "Praise God'' for a mother's love.

Fixing my hair every two weeks had already become an overwhelming responsibility for my mother. Hot combing someone's hair was very stressful. Most of this stress was generated from trying to straighten the edges and to get that "kitchen" right. It could seem like you were walking through the valley of the Shadow of Death. You were told to hold your head perfectly still so the hot comb would not burn you. I quickly learned this sitting perfectly still business didn't guarantee you would come through this ordeal without getting burned. I would, however, agree that your chances of not getting burned were a lot better if you didn't flinch or act like you had a tick whenever the hot comb came near your neck or ear.

It was extremely frustrating for my mother to do my hair because I behaved like I had Tourette Syndrome every time I sat near the stove. The skillset of the straighter has to be one hundred because no matter how much she pulled at my hair it never stretched any longer than the distance from that hot comb to the end of my neck. To build confidence and correctly straighten someone's hair that is short and tightly coiled you needed a very small hot comb and a large hot comb, not just that Frankenstein monster of a hot comb my mother had. After a few episodes of my unreasonable fear of the hot comb, and the great amount of resistance my hair put forth to being straightened, my mother was through wrestling with it. She complained times were hard but decided I needed a professional at my side and was willing to pay for it. My mother said, "Look, life is too short for me to be putting up with all this damn aggravation every time I try to straighten that nappy hair of yours. I'm sick of you and your hair."

Squabbles about Black hair could make decent people resort to physical violence. My father got dinged on the head because he said my mother's hair had never been as good as my sister's hair. My mother was adamantly trying to defend her "good" hair of yesteryear but alas there were no pictures to prove her statements. All she really had was "The Story". I believed my mother's story because her hair was past her shoulders and very thick. It just required quite a bit of straightening with a very hot comb. A trick Black hair is famous for is changing its texture as you grow older or due to the weather. Most Black men were not aware of this and did not care that Black hair could change its properties over a period of time. My father's refusal to agree to the fact my mother had "good hair" at one time turned a discussion into a very heated argument. Apparently, my father had no idea how important it was for our mother to be in the hierarchy of the good hair women's club. My father kept up his assault on her hair until my mother violently threw a hard, thick, glass hairbrush at my father's head that TKO'd my dad and made him fall back onto the couch. Needless to say, no one in my family ever again debated my mother about her position in the good hair women's club.

Because of overcrowding in the seventh grade, I went to an all-girls high school, what a privilege. I was fascinated by how sophisticated the older girls behaved. All-day long, many fashions that made my mouth water, were paraded up and down the halls. At night I would practice wearing heels. I laid out my most grown-up clothes hoping to be mistaken for one of the high school girls. The only thing holding me back from my total fashion statement was a beehive hairdo. The Beehive hairstyle looked as if you had a pillbox hat on your head. The pillbox hat was the latest style because Jacqueline Kennedy, the first lady of the United States. She wore the pillbox hat. That weekend my mother had gotten my hair done at the salon and it was super straight. While the hairdresser was doing my hair, I was calculating my beehive plan. Finally, Monday afternoon came, and I stopped by the store and got all the tools that were needed for the hairstyle. I felt so grown up at the store when I ordered all of the Beehive hair utensils. I purchased hairspray, hairpins, and a long rat tail comb to tease my hair into the perfect Beehive. Well, I learned that day the true meaning of "The best-laid plans of mice and men often go awry." That afternoon all was going well. My parents were working, and my sister was outside doing things that children do. I, on the other hand, was born to create and live in the limelight of the fashion world. I had gotten some direction on how to style my hair in a beehive from one of the older students at school. But after what happened, I realized unfortunately that hairspray's first ingredient is water, and the second ingredient is sticky glue. First, I teased all of my hair and had it standing on top of my head. Perhaps if I had only used a very little hair spray all might not have been lost. My hair was standing upright but I decided that it should be harder to the touch. Then suddenly, my hair started to do what it does when too much water comes into contact with Black hair that has just been pressed with a hot comb. My hair shriveled up before my very eyes. My entire beehive project had gone south.

Have you ever had a project you really wanted to be successful, but no matter how hard you tried to save your project it just continued to spiral down the drain until you were left trying to make something out of nothing? I had turned my hair into a bee's nest that was now glued to the top of my head. My first mistake was thinking I could accomplish the Beehive hairstyle with my texture of hair. My second mistake was I had no formal training in hairdressing. My hairstyling skillset was extremely low. Once my mother arrived home, she reiterated those facts quite clearly until it was crystal clear to me and everyone in the house. I know she wanted to slap me into next week when she thought about how foolish I had been to destroy that recently purchased twenty-dollar hairdo. Over the years, my mother and I would have quite a few painful experiences regarding my hair. Inevitably I always suffered the consequences of my foolish actions because I knew more than anyone the least bit of humidity would cause my hair to transform into a giant Brillo pad.

What in the world would make me saturate and tease my hair with a sticky watery solution and expect anything other than the nasty mess that sat upon my head? I don't know what upset my mother more, my desire for such an adult hairstyle or that I used a hair product with the main ingredients being water and glue. I don't know if her anger was because of how many blouses she had to stand on her feet and iron to make twenty dollars that I had now wasted due to my stupidity or if it was because she had to struggle with my hair for the next three hours before she could go to bed. Or, most importantly, was she upset because I had such a desperate desire to be something other than who I was? I can tell you this... before I went to bed that night my mother and I explored each of the above scenarios quite extensively! In my mind I was an adult in a child's body, so my troubles were always complicated. God, please give me and my mother strength.

Unless you have good Black hair, you will require a lot of care to make it look fabulous. To achieve great hairstyles when you have regular Black hair can be an illusion that requires hard work and hours of preparation. One morning, I saw my mother break down in tears because I had not tied my new hairstyle upon going to bed after she had just spent money to have this illusion performed. To this very day, I will not sleep with a scarf on my head. I always feel like it cuts off the circulation to my head which gives me nightmares.

Over the years, beauty products for Black hair have become a huge megabuck industry. The American cosmetic and beauty business saw just how much money women were willing to pay for products they believe would transform them into who they saw on TV. Once again, the White cosmetic industry fools the Black woman into believing she too could have carefree hair just like a White woman. Black women wanted to go to sleep without having to set their hair every night or having to use a hot curler to maintain a head full of curls. Black women desperately wanted and needed something that would set them free from the drudgery of accomplishing the illusion of pretty hair. Hair companies were always researching, and marketing products geared toward the Black woman. A commercial is a group of words so skillfully spoken about a product that it becomes crucial to have because it is the ultimate answer for all of your problems. Once again, Black women, wanting to be set free from all the work of Black hair, are fooled into believing a miracle from the White businessman. The manufacturing world had come up with a magic potion for Black hair. It was just like what White women used and it was not a grease but a gel. Oh, happy day!!

My first experience with this new wonder gel product was when my mother was attending a bus ride to the country. Since we lived in a city project there was a real need to get out into the open air and allow your feet to touch real grass that a dog had not messed in. These bus rides were expensive and were a big to-do in the projects. White folks made plenty of money transporting Black people who lived in the city and longed to see trees and smell sweet green grass, if only for one lousy day. Preparation for these bus outings usually required about a month or so to get right. Your outfit had to be fine yet comfortable. Quite frankly, only the elite people could spend that kind of money for a one-day outing. My mother was an attractive curvy woman with beautiful hair, so it was very important to her that her hair was super fabulous. The night before the bus outing she asked me to roll her hair with that miracle gel and it was going to make her hair do what it does. My mother told me how to use this gel and since she had such thick hair, I saturated it pretty good. She said the more the better. Well, were we ever wrong with a capital W! My mother wanted to be on time when her friends arrived for their outing, so I got up extra early to fry chicken and make potato salad for her lunch and of course help with her hair. They were leaving at 7:00 am and since the work in the kitchen involved steam there was no need to take out her rollers. The steam might have loosened up her curls too much. Well, that morning we were going to have some serious troubles, but loose curls would not be one of them. Now that the food was made, and the lunch was packed it was time to get dressed and take the rollers out of her hair. In the famous words of Rod

Sterling, we had just entered the twilight zone of gel. As I took out each roller, every curl stood straight up and resembled a stiff block of wood. I had never seen anything like it before. I immediately realized the gel had done something awful to her hair but at that moment I was too afraid to say anything. Each curl resisted vehemently to join the other curls on her head. They all wanted to stay separated like an island unto themselves. The comb nor the brush had no real effect on the curls, so I got the afro pick and started to pick her hair. Then each strand of hair wanted to be an island. I was overcome by nervousness, but I wanted to laugh so badly that tears started to swell in my eyes. But because I feared for my life, not even a whimper came from my lips. My mother's friends would be at the door in the next ten minutes and her hair was going to require way more attention than ten minutes. We had to think fast but we were in the Twilight Zone of that watery gel and rational thinking was not a part of this game. This was something we knew nothing about. My mother tried to make a ponytail which would have been fine, but her hair was too thick for the rubber band, so it popped, and her hair immediately went back to its original state. Finally, I suggested some stiff hair grease because I thought that might tame her hair down enough and allow us to gain some control. We worked with her hair until we made a curly Afro which she did not want but we had no choice. By the time she returned home late that evening, her hair looked like Angela Davis on a bad hair day. We continued to use this watery gel product, but you had to make some concessions by using it sparingly and of course, and along with the old landmark Dixie Peach hair pomade for real the Black women.

This hair shriveling situation brings to mind another time my hair betrayed me with a horrible outcome. I met a fine young guy named Nate at a Drum and Bugle Corps party. I have always been attracted to a man in a uniform. Unfortunately, most men in uniform are usually whores because so many women are fascinated with the uniform. It has to be those shiny buttons and doodads decorating the uniform that probably reminds them of appliances. Believe me, you would have gotten much more service and satisfaction from an appliance than sitting by the phone waiting for that negro in a uniform to make his occasional booty call. "Lord give me strength." Nate was really built due to all that marching and carrying a huge drum and believe me he knew how to beat that drum. He was promoted to lead drummer in record time. Nate had good hair. It was jet black with thick, natural, deep waves. I loved spreading my fingers in between his waves. It was like laying your hands on a fine piano. Nate's naturally wavy, fine hair and those shiny buttons on that well-fitting uniform had women, all over Brooklyn and the Bronx, on assignment for his attention. To my surprise and delight, he was very attentive to me and took me out every chance he got.

Nate's brother did not resemble him or his mother so I assumed he must have had a different father. This brother had a girlfriend that was a real live sea monster with measly hair, but I heard she had a sister that could steal time. Therefore, the sea monster was always in the very latest fashions. It was obvious Nate's brother enjoyed being seen with a girl that could dress well. That duo, however, had met its match because Nate and I had all things working. We were both fine, and with my mother's hard-earned money paying that growing hand hairdresser, my hair had grown to be shoulder length. I had a fabulous shape and a wild imagination for fashion. With lots of practicing on the sewing machine, my skill set was 100 percent even on a bad day. The sea monster's stolen outfits were lost in my glamour because I was wearing and slaying outfits they just didn't have in stores.

Nate always insisted on hanging out with his brother and his girlfriend. I too had become a part of this sick competition. Nate's brother's girlfriend had bought all four of us tickets to a ball for a Black-owned newspaper but did not tell us until the day of the event. I know her secret agenda was to be totally prepared and really show out in a beautiful dress. I had to work fast. I got my hairdresser to change my appointment from

Saturday morning to Friday afternoon because I was taking no chances. Well, I was truly done. I had my hair beat to a T. It was like Diana Ross' famous side swoop that hung to the bottom of my neck and you know dear sisters this is before weaves. The girlfriend did her absolute best, and she did look nice, but she could not touch my hairdo or my outfit. Nate and I must have danced every record fast and slow we just had to dance. We were after all in a competition. Well, you know that slow grind dancing can do some terrible things to your hair especially if your partner's face has the least bit of perspiration. I never liked alcohol but the two drinks I had along with all that gusto dancing produced way more sweat than my hair could endure without making drastic changes to its appearance. I was really going hard at it, doing the Hustle, and grinding it up for all I was worth. All the while unaware my hair was dancing just as hard as I was with disastrous results. During the ball, Nate and I were like the king and queen of the Prom. I thought I was so very cute. We were laughing, talking and I was acting out all the latest project gossip stories for my audience with my own special drama. It was now time to go home, and I just happened to catch a glimpse of my hair. I was horrified. My knees went limp, and I actually stumbled causing me to grab out to catch Nate's arm. That side sweep I was so proud of early on in the evening was now securely affixed to almost the top of my head. The rest of my hair had reverted to its natural state of steel wool and the Jewish side dangling curls were now just nappy blocks of hair on the sides of my face. I was like Cinderella at midnight when all of her lovely props reverted to what they once were. But this was so much worse because I was really living this tragedy. Then I instantly thought about how cute I was acting with a picky head and all the while the sea monster must have been enjoying every minute of my humiliating performance. I did not know any of these girls at the ball so there was no one to pull my coat tail about my hair's transformation. By the time I got in the cab I couldn't speak which was a big change because earlier that evening all I could do was talk. I'm not the type to get headaches, but this embarrassment went straight to my head and caused one of the worst headaches I've ever had. Nate wanted to make out in the cab, but I told him my head was really hurting which was the gospel truth.

I Know Everything

Being ugly in America is a terrible thing as a child. You are teased, tormented, and suffer a sad life. It is a dark world I know first-hand because I was an ugly child. I thank God during my grade school years I lived on a small block in Brooklyn. If I had lived in a large city project in my early years, I would not have survived. To make matters worse, my sister who was only a year younger was an extremely beautiful child. I didn't realize I was afflicted with such a curse until about the age of seven. It was also about that time my mother let me know I did not have good hair! My mother told me in no uncertain terms my hair would require an extremely hot comb and because of the type of hair I possessed, White America would be hard-pressed to find me attractive. She also went on to say, White people associated my nappy hair texture with slavery, and none of them wanted that type of reminder in the workplace. She said if I were going to be a cleaning woman perhaps my type of hair would be more palatable. But since being a cleaning woman wasn't her plan for my life, I would have to learn to endure the dreaded hot comb.

She summed up my hair lesson by telling me the only people who wouldn't mind my hair being a nappy texture, were White women with long, beautiful hair. Because in their minds, nappy hair made me invisible and no competition to their fair beauty. But when it comes right down to the mat, a White woman's long hair doesn't amount to a hill of beans compared to the big ample behind most sister's strut. That big sexy behind conjures many sensual images in a man's head, and most of those images have nothing to do with hair, and everything to do with what it's like to roll around with that big behind. I will go into greater detail about the Black women's hair struggles as well as that big ample behind most sisters are blessed to have. But for now, let's get back to life as an ugly child.

Until the age of seven, I lived under the sole protection of my home life. I lived as an older sister to a beautiful little sister and never felt the bitter truth of being an extremely ugly duckling. My parents were deceived by those loving eyes that only parents have concerning their children. Being ugly is a true nightmare where you live in real-time in front of a live audience. This nightmare had many scenarios that only came to one conclusion. I was truly ugly, and my sister was truly beautiful. What really had most people's hair on fire was they had no way to disprove my claim that beyond a shadow of a doubt this adorable child was my sister. If it were at all possible, they would have DNA tested me on the spot for having such nerve to even say I could possibly be close kin to someone so beautiful. I believed in the eyes of most people, I was Quasimodo and should be banished to the woodland on the outskirts of town. And if I knew where the woodland on the outskirts of town was, I would have run there in order to stop the hurt.

Every new person I met in the company of my sister reacted the same way. With utter amazement regarding my looks compared to my dear sister. Children say what they think, but I also had to endure the many adults that expressed their feelings about my awful situation. Now, I must admit there were quite a few problems with my physical make up. For example, I was extremely thin and had a striking resemblance to a stick figure. My head was very large but somehow, I had a small face. I inherited my father's large nose and my mother's very full lips. I had short measly hair, and two front teeth that would have rivaled Bugs Bunny. If a situation room really exists, then I was in it playing hardball without a catcher's mitt. Fortunately for me, the only mercy I received from this constant torment came in a most unusual way. My best friend Sandy who was blind.

Sandy never knew my dilemma and I never cared about hers. We both benefited from this relationship remarkably and strangely. Sandy taught me to read at a very early age. My friend was four years older than I and her mother insisted I practice brail with her. I managed to get older reader books from school, and I would follow along while she read aloud to me. I learned to read quite well at the tender age of seven but the only books that really caught my interest were "True Love Confessions" and adult erotic love stories. My mother was furious with my literary choices, but I continued to read them behind her back.

I did notice whenever my parents were around other people the adults in the room managed to compose themselves regarding my looks. I instantly realized if I were grown the horrible assaults on my looks would end. It never dawned on me that my face would eventually accommodate my large striking features. I just knew if I were an adult this horrendous nightmare would end. The same people who had been so cruel to me as a child would now use their grownup manners and be satisfied with the pleasure of talking behind my back. There was another upside to the whole matter of being grown. I wouldn't have to spend all my waking hours constantly being compared to my lovely sister. Praise the living God!

Since my looks were such a constant source of misery it drove me to become obsessed with being grown. Our minds are the most powerful tool on earth. Just imagine how prisons have all this technology at hand but prisoners constantly outsmart them using only their brains. The brain controls the entire body and thinking back I believe my mind is what brought my period on at the early age of nine years old. I was constantly trying to prove to everyone around me I was much older than my chronological age. I was forever plotting and planning scenarios that would show me in a more grown up light. After reading all those steamy love stories, I knew just how young adult women were supposed to behave.

At an incredibly young age, I began watching, no, the real term would be studying the "I Love Lucy" show. I loved the way Lucy was able to influence everyone around her as well as any situation she encountered. Respectful love came from family, friends, and even strangers as Lucy solved the most complicated predicaments with elegance and humor. Once puberty started, I made every effort to become Jacqueline Kennedy and Lucy. Whatever the situation called for, these two women were always winners, and everyone loves a winner. I finally realized this head God had given me was truly not meant for beauty. Besides, everyone had made a conscious effort to make me well aware of that. I knew the Lord had blessed me with an exceptional mind. Therefore, I would make good use of this large head for making money.

Until adulthood, all my brainstorming would be hindered by a lack of money and those who had power over me. I already acted grownup. Now all I needed were props such as clothes and makeup. Not that my mother would allow me to wear these things, but I could always talk my girlfriends into playing dress-up. My friends would beg and borrow things from their older sisters and mothers and bring them to my house. I would then trade or sell my toys for these clothing items. I had figured out a way to have my very own dress-up clothes. I had quite the collection of grown-up props, including eyeliner, lipstick, and mascara. But all of these items took careful planning to obtain on my part. Quite often, I was allowed to go shopping with my older cousin because when my mother got home from work, she was worn out. I would then use the money from my lucrative toy sales to purchase makeup. Once at the tender age of ten, my father heard me speaking with another girl my age and it seemed to him I was manipulating her out of her money. I quickly informed him she so wanted the paper dolls I was selling because due to her carelessness, she now had none. I also let him know the price for my paper dolls was only a mere fraction of the cost they were in the store. I told my father I saw Lucy and Ethel raise money for a fundraiser when they needed money to go on a trip. He then told me to be careful and not to cheat anyone. I assured him my friend received an allowance every week and by no means was I taking advantage of her.

I believed in my dreams and I knew I would appear to be more adult-like with the right props. So, I had to be very strict with myself and resist taking my toys out of their boxes. If I was going to get top dollar for these items sacrifices had to be made. My grown-up attitude gave me the resistance to never play with the toys I received at Christmas. I had the ability to wheel and deal and it made me light years above all the children my age. Whenever I sold a toy or anything else for that matter, I would get the price the market could bear. My secret life of being grown ruled my entire waking hours. I always had quite a few bright ideas going on at one time. All of my "Lucy like" schemes were really cooking! They involved Christmas toys, birthday presents, paper, and plastic dolls, or any other childlike item I could get top dollar for. I had no interest in these items other than their ability to make me money!

I carefully stored these trinkets and brought them out in February when all the girls had gotten their dolls dirty or had destroyed their other toys. Back in the day, children received an allowance for doing their chores and as my good fortune would have it, quite a few girls received weekly allowances in my neighborhood. I don't know if these people were affluent, but apparently, they had more money than my family enjoyed. They tell me success depends on preparation and I was prepared! I had lovely paper dolls and a variety of other toys that would bring cold hard cash. These transactions allowed me to literally stockpile all types of makeup, beauty supplies, and grown-up props.

I lived on a small block in Brooklyn where the people were very slow. On the surface, marriages were like God intended. Women stayed home and men came home from their job at six. Good girls had steady boyfriends, and if the fickle finger of fate got confused and a raincoat was not used, she of course got pregnant. The boy then usually had to pay for that box in full. It could not be put on layaway, nor was it cheap. A man was made to pay with his very life. The price tag for that forbidden fruit was marriage. I knew life was much more than what these nice people were showing me, and I was created to discover all their little dirty grown-up secrets.

The most exciting thing I did during this time was Tuesday night fireworks at Coney Island. Now, I have to admit there were a few downsides to these Tuesday night excursions. My family was carless, so I devised a plan to get my sister and me invitations to my best friend's family Tuesday night firework events. Every Tuesday night I told my parents we had been expressly invited by my girlfriend's parents to accompany them on these wonderful outings. I did enjoy seeing the fireworks, but I simply loved being out in the city at night just like an adult. My parents must have known these people didn't invite two extra children with very little money on an outing that could become quite costly. But my parents were without a car and they saw how much we enjoyed the outings. The excitement of how happy my sister and I were to go to Coney Island must have made my parents turn a blind eye to the whole situation. Thinking back, it also must have been wonderful for a young couple like my parents to be rid of our prying eyes and ears for at least five hours. While enjoying those Nathan hot dogs, I finally figured out it had to be the wonderful night ocean air that made those Nathan hot dogs so tasty when they popped in your mouth. The pleasure of that hot dog was almost stolen away by my girlfriend's mother's insensitive remark. She said, and I quote "This outing is killing my pocketbook!" Nevertheless, she took us the very next week, so I attributed it to a small buyer's regret and moved on. The Bible says, when you make something possible for the least of them, we do it unto Him. Therefore, I was very happy for this woman to get a blessing.

As a child, I always managed to listen intently to every adult conversation. In my heart of hearts, I knew these people were living hot, passionate lives they kept under the covers, and I mean that literally. However, this was not an easy task. The adults had a strict code of conduct and rule number one was never talk grownup business in front of children. My parents tried their very best to follow these rules, but they had no idea how my desire to be an adult mandated my entire existence. They were no match for me. At five years old in private, I practiced how my every action, conversation, and even my physical appearance would display how grown up I really was. Listening to adult conversations was my life's blood. Every weekend I turned into a silent hunter tracking down every juicy bit of adult gossip that was in the air. To my good fortune, I had a big advantage over the adults. I drank no alcohol, and I had a finicky appetite during that time in my life. I never gored myself with food so the adults could not feed me and send me off to bed thinking I would fall asleep on a full stomach. I required very little sleep. Unfortunately for them, when they got together on weekends, they drank, they ate, and did they talk!!!. As I stated before, luck is always with the prepared. Alcohol had loosened their tongues and their cardinal rule was now null and void! I used to take out a large paper doll book and pretended to be playing. All the while, I was listening to their every word.

Once, I heard my mother say a neighbor lived with a man and that "She is lucky to have him take on the responsibility of her five children because they are not his kids." This was so intriguing to me. Who did the children belong to? Who was their biological father? I decided to do some inquiries about who this mystery man was. Needless to say, it was a big mistake. I decided to start my investigation with some of the children in the neighborhood. They assured me of their discretion in this delicate matter. But of course, the story was just too juicy for anyone to keep to themselves. I told them the entire story I overheard from my mother and her friends when they were discussing this mystery man. This story was so big, I decided to add a special attraction. I did my mother's voice and acted out the conversation to make the story more interesting and entertaining. Within an hour, my investigation had gone terribly wrong. The children I took into my confidence to find the mystery man's identity immediately started to tease our neighbor's children. These cruel children went on to tell them the man their mother lived with was not their father. Of course, this shocking story of such excessive immorality caused all the women in the neighborhood to take a moment and clutch their pearls while steading themselves. This was a most devastating story and it caused bitter tears for children and angry words for adults. The unlucky woman in question was now the talk of the entire neighborhood and she also had the difficult task of trying to console her very distraught children. Needless to say, my mother was extremely upset with me and physically showed me her take on this wretched matter. It was truly a sad day for me. I was reprimanded and beaten just like a naughty child which was the cruelest punishment of all for me.

My parents moved up in life by taking an apartment in the Marcy Projects. When I met the Marcy Projects, I was twelve years old entering the amazing world of becoming a teenager. A rush of emotions swept over me the first time I saw the new place I would call home. I stepped on the project grounds with keen anticipation. I was "Feelin Alright" just like Mr. Joe Cocker would say in the coming years. I had too much to do before I died, and I knew my life had just begun.

The little block I came from was light years behind the Marcy Projects. The Marcy Projects was composed of 27 buildings. All of the buildings had six floors with a combined total of 1,705 apartments. They say 4,286 people lived in the Marcy Projects. That meant 4,286 people had the potential to be my friends, enemies, or just sons of a guns sent from the pits of hell to pull me down. The Marcy Projects was a city where the struggle was real. If you failed at achieving your life's dreams, you would be a permanent resident of the Marcy Houses. Success had to be always on your mind. I learned to keep my "to-go-bag" and papers updated. Ready to transition from that rock'n'roll crab barrel called the Marcy Projects to a higher level in life with the least amount of effort.

In 1963, I was twelve years old. If Google had been in existence they would have used me for "Hey Siri '' because I thought I knew everything. I was working with a few special facts that assured me I was the number one candidate for "Hey Siri." I was living in the ghetto capital of Brooklyn. A housing project notorious for its fast and dangerous life. Also, I was being groomed for this life of stardom by the best teachers known to the free world Motown. I knew in my heart I had the favor of God supporting me with my mission to be an educated diva. Also, at the age of twelve I had eagle eyes which gave me a discerning woman's spirit. Therefore, I was able to make something out of nothing. In my mind's eye, I saw fashion trends way ahead of my girlfriends. I could take two dollars' worth of material and make a sensual outfit that no man of any age could resist. This impressive trick was accomplished by me lying and conniving my way into a high school extracurricular activities club. These clubs were for the older girls that desired home economic classes that taught sewing and hat making. While other girls my age were still playing with dolls, or home watching Bozo the clown, I was getting busy changing myself into a sophisticated diva. My goal was to be a ghetto, Jacklyn Kennedy. I wore Pillbox hats and made Vogue suits from patterns I learned to make right there at the sewing club. I felt Jacklyn Kennedy and I had an allegiance. We both looked good in those Ray

Charles dark sunglasses and since my mother's family name was Kennedy that sealed the deal for me.

I knew in my heart and soul it was not my karma to be stuck in a long-drawn-out childhood. I had my period since I was nine, I was still a virgin with no desire for children and I was preparing myself in various ways to attain a rich ghetto fabulous reputation. To do so, my pillbox hats and designer suits were a must and of course, I made them myself. I was not as sharp as the arrow but when the arrow flew by me I made him stop!! and say without hesitation this chick is sharp. My ducks were in a straight row which I knew gave me great leeway over most girls my age.

I was twelve, my sister was ten and we were now surrounded by young teenage girls who lived in adoration of other young girls, who were teen moms with their own budgets that came directly from the Department of Social Services. My first week in the Marcy my sister and I met fine young Black and Puerto Rican boys, who were itching to play house. Life was really good. The first party my sister and I attended had no theme and the lights were out on the dance floor. Despite our strong protest, my mother insisted we take a present to a party that was not celebrating anything in particular and she dressed us in those baby organdy dresses. Our new friend's mother, the hostess of this get together loved us because finally someone brought some class to this whore- in- training- party.

The girls in the projects gave my sister and me the lay of the land. This of course meant them telling us everybody's business. Miss Brown, a woman of a good age, had just spent two years in jail for performing illegal abortions. I heard she was pretty good. Better than a dirty back alley with knitting needles. To my utter surprise, I was also told her doing time was like water rolling off a duck's back because for five hundred dollars she was still available. No one ever said she was even a nurse's aide. It was just said she knew her way around the vagina and uterus pretty good. Life in the Marcy taught me early on to never judge any of these books by their covers. Make no mistake, that dollar, that filthy lucre was afraid of nothing. The number of people in the projects that had a mental illness diagnosis was staggering. Between a Medicaid psychiatrist and the local drug dealer, these were people on the edge. Once these patients grew weary of the doctors along with self-medication to compose themselves, they depended on Motown's music to stop their madness. At any given time one of those crazy clowns could get confused and kill you. Before your family even had time to raise the money to bury your unfortunate behind, some egotistical state psychiatrist would deem the accused cured of all mental illnesses and all wrongdoing. This mentally ill patient had been given a get out of jail free card. Your best bet in the city of the Marcy asylum was to pray earnestly that the Lord thy God bless and keep you. Because there was no real safety in the man-made institutional law and order.

I had not been living in the Marcy Projects long before I started to endure many embarrassing moments. Most of the time, they weren't really my fault. I have always loved animals, especially dogs. I believed I was sent here to be their savior. Unfortunately, my fear of them didn't allow me to save any of them. I would soon find out that the Marcy had many more dogs than I was used to. Where I'd come from, I knew all the dogs in the neighborhood on a first name basis. I love dogs but I am terrified of any dog if we have not been properly introduced because those types of encounters usually go horribly wrong. During my very early years in the Marcy, there were quite a few dog chasings. One of these episodes caused the police to be involved. I saw a dog, we made eye contact, and instantly, he started to chase me. He chased me right into an old couple's home whose door was slightly ajar. Unfortunately, the door didn't close behind me, and the dog who was hard on my heels came in also. I was hysterical! In the confusion, I tripped over the old lady's cane and fell into her lap. The old lady was screaming I'd broken into their home and her husband immediately called the police. While scrambling to get away from the dog the only sanctuary I saw was their bedroom and I managed to close that door behind me. While I took refuge in the old lady's bedroom, she was demanding I come out, but the dog was still barking, and I was too afraid to open the door. The police finally arrive, and they open the bedroom door and I'm doing my very best to explain the situation in my scared state. Unfortunately, my story might have been more credible if the dog weighed more than twenty pounds soaking wet. The dog is now licking the policeman's hand, and I have lost all trustworthiness. My story of being chased by a vicious dog was not being well received. The woman is still furious, and to make matters worse, the woman's neighbor, who happens to be the dog's owner, is at the door. She can hear her dog barking and wants to know why her sweet little dog is in her neighbor's home. Supposedly, the dog was out to pee and when I made eye contact with him and ran, he quite naturally chased me. The dog probably hadn't had that much fun in years. When my mother arrived, she did her very best to explain to everyone how I could have possibly been afraid of such a small friendly dog. But alas, the story doesn't end here. The old couple's home was a very small, cramped apartment with huge animal statues in every corner. Because I was running around like a maniac, I accidentally broke one of the old lady's animal statues. I had bumped into a tiger statue and its head popped right off its shoulders. Years later, my mother and I thought about that tiger's head and how even the break was with no jagged edges. We now believe it had been previously broken before, probably by her husband but I had been the perfect scapegoat.

Another incident with a dog ended with my entire coat sleeve being ripped off. This particular day I had been sent on one of the most dreaded errands of my young teenage days, so I was already terribly upset. My sister suffered from severe menstrual cramps, so my mother sent me to purchase medicine for cramps and a large box of menstrual pads by the brand name of Modess. From outside of the drug store, I can immediately see this is not going to be good because the place is full of people of all genders, ages, and nationalities. The pharmacist of course is drooling from all the potential money that now stands before him and his cash register. He and his young male assistant behind the counter were up on a platform with their superiority firmly established. My turn finally came but I couldn't bring myself to ask for the box of Modess. I did try to say the name of the product without saying the word menstrual or pads, but the pharmacist became quite annoyed with me. His only interest in life was selling, not deciphering the marbles in my mouth. He decided the quick way to get to the next customer was to be rid of me fast and in a hurry. So, in a loud mean voice, he yelled at me and said, "Do not return here until you've learned how to talk young lady." I ran out of the drug store in shame. The pharmacist never missed a beat. In the same breath, he asked the next customer how he could help them. I had two options, go back into the drug store, and face that hateful pharmacist or go to the supermarket where I could probably run into many more people with my large economy size box of Modess. To top it all off, there was a good size dog that sometimes hung around the supermarket begging for food. My God, it was an awful day. I opted to go to the supermarket and take my chances being seen with that large box of pads, and perhaps lady luck would smile upon me and that dog would have died. But of course, as Murphy law would have it that dog was alive and well at his attack post. He immediately came out at me. He was growling and snarling and jumped at my hand which I quickly pulled up into my sleeve. I tried to get away, but he had the low ground and a four-paw advantage. At that moment, the dog seemed to be doing a little dance as we engaged in this violent tug of war. The dog appeared to be enjoying this to the max and I could tell this was not his first rodeo. Once he grew weary of the tug of war and decided he had toyed with me long enough. He let out a big ferocious bark and took a huge gulp of my sleeve which tore right off my coat at the shoulder seam. To tell the truth, I was relieved just to be rid of him. At that moment I didn't care about that sleeve. I was just elated to have my entire hand. I was so busy trying to save my hand fighting with that dog that I didn't see the boys at the corner of the grocery store laughing so hard they had fallen to the ground. Thank God they composed themselves long enough to run after that hound from hell and return my coat sleeve. When the boys ran after the dog he was a real coward. He put up no resistance. He dropped my sleeve immediately, tucked his tail, and ran away as fast as his four feet could carry him.

I got home and all hell broke loose as the sleeve of my new jacket was in my hand. My mother started fussing and said, "You must purposely be antagonizing these dogs or you're actually a cat in disguise!" Whatever the case, she told me she was not made of money and I had better figure out a way to attach that sleeve back onto my jacket. The jacket and sleeve situation had barely blown over when my sister pipes up and starts complaining about having to tear sheets to make sanitary napkins. This of course starts my mother again about where was the large box of Modess she had sent me for. During my tussle with the dog, I somehow lost most of the money. My mother and sister weren't happy, but I was really glad to be home. I knew my girlfriend and I would fix my jacket because she was going to high school to be a tailor. And most importantly, I had my hand and my arm, which I would use to tear up sheets into sanitary napkins. Life was good.

My burning desire to be above all the ordinary girls in the projects was an obsession of mine day and night. I decided college would be my avenue to accomplish my goals. Let me tell every woman in the free world to dream for greatness because it is in you. Anything or person that would interfere with my dream of being a cut above had to be eliminated at once before it took a foot whole of my dreams. At my all-girls high school, a few girls followed a strict religious sect. They wore prayer cloths on their heads every day and dresses that swept the floor. I met one of these girls after high school with four children and one in the oven and of course no husband. Before I knew it, I said, "Girl you should have had that prayer cloth over that fertile box of yours where it might have done some good." We both laughed, but I was serious. Four children and one on the way would be a real setback to anyone's future.

The projects were like a vacuum. It accepted all new things, good or bad. The government came out with a plan for poor people to receive health care in New York state and it was called Medicaid. People in the projects jumped on the Medicaid program immediately. They were relieved to avoid that six to twelve-hour wait and maybe even death in a hospital emergency room. The local doctor's office was so convenient and finally, all the hassle of the emergency waiting room was eliminated. A White doctor or a Black doctor which usually meant he has a White man's psyche saw the Medicaid program as the ultimate vehicle to millionaire status. Across the street from the projects near the liquor and grocery store, a doctor went from one lone office to a strip mall which practiced all the poor man's specialties: diabetes, arthritis, heart disease, blood pressure, mental health, obstetrics, and gynecology. There was of course, the family practitioner for all the other little worries. This medical center was like the gift that kept on giving. No official Id was required, only the presentation of a Medicaid card. Once this card had been presented it was only required to make its appearance once a year. Enterprising poor people managed to make money with the Medicaid program because they would rent someone their card for an office visit or even large ticket items such as abortions. You see all things were working in this Medicaid scheme.

I had an obsession to stay a perfect size 10, but I also had an obsession with inhaling food at every meal.

The amount of food I seemed to require could easily have fed a family of three. I tried to throw up after eating, but I can tell you that is not for the faint of heart. A huge amount of food does not easily come up without the body naturally rejecting the content of your stomach. I had to take this awful medicine so I could throw up with force and once it did come up it was a terrible ordeal. The food came up in large chunks out of my mouth and nose. After a while, I thought it was trying to come through my ears. This violent action made my head go into a tailspin. My head hurt for hours afterwards. My career as a bulimic was cut short. I never looked back at that method to lose weight. I was desperately seeking another way to keep my weight down when I met this older girl. I admired her body and she said for five dollars a visit I could use her Medicaid card. I was delighted. She told me to go to the crazy doctor because the family doctor would only give prescriptions for weak diet pills. I had to only inform the doctor I was always tired and could barely study for my nurse's aide course. A smart Black person knew that some White people never wanted to hear about a Black person advancing too much or they may not be so happy to help. So, the nurse's aide course would do nicely.

The crazy doctor only came once a week, but I was told he would write you a two-month prescription. I was disappointed at first when I called to see what day he would be at the clinic. I was told the doctor was not accepting any new patients. Can you imagine a Medicaid doctor not accepting new patients? That's the laugh of the century. But then I remembered I grew up with one of the "play-play" Puerto Rican nurses that worked in the office. She said, "Don't worry about it, I'll fit you in the doctor's schedule even if I have to bump someone else out." On the day of my appointment, I saw why the doctor wasn't accepting new patients. There wasn't even standing room in his office. It was a total scary zoo. Over the years the projects had shown me many things. I had become accustomed to it so my fear level in the ghetto was extremely low. But what was going at this doctor's office was up close and way too personal. There were heroin addicts, cocaine addicts, speed ballers, and of course the all-time favorite alcoholics. The cocaine addicts couldn't stop talking or sweating and could have easily drenched a large bath towel. The speed ballers couldn't stay still and seemed to be suffering from a severe case of Tourette's Syndrome. The heroin addicts were the most pitiful lot. Some had missed their veins and now had huge mammoth arms and hands with open large sores draining pus. You know I must have really wanted those prescriptions or thought little of my life to go to such a dangerous place. Everyone in the office hated me because I was not in the same condition. No one ever took their eyes off of my pocketbook. You would think they could magically open it with their eyes. At any moment, a terrible fight could break out and someone could lose their life.

What I was not prepared for was the doctor. He was frail, ninety-five-year-old with a very weak voice. The doctor could barely slide his feet behind the walker that his grandson helped him hold on to as they entered the office. I would have bet money and borrowed some that the doctor was going to die before he finished with his very first patient. Looking at him, I was beside myself with worry that I was not going to get my prescription that day. There were about sixty of us in that tiny office and I was surprised I did not catch tuberculosis. This went on for about eight months. Every time I showed up for my office visit, he actually looked worse than the last time I saw him. But on this particular visit, he frightened me. I kept thinking he could possibly die and where would I get these pills from because now I was a perfect size ten. For some reason, I felt the need to express my concerns to him. I thought perhaps he would take better care of himself. I told him I was terrified, and he said very gently "What's wrong my dear?" I said, "You are so old. I am afraid you might die any minute." He and his grandson instantly became furious! Like I had said something they never thought of before. The doctor told me "Get out!" and I was never to come back again. I was most fortunate because I already had my prescription in hand. I told the girl who had lent me the Medicaid card what happened, and she thought it was hilarious. But I needed my pills to stay a size ten. She told me to calm down because Fort Greene had another doctor with a Medicaid empire only twenty minutes away. All was not lost.

Not having had any sexual experience and being five years into this period thing, my hormones were starting to talk loud and clear at certain times of the month. Now, what was I going to do about this dilemma? I wanted nothing to do with masturbation. It always seemed so needy and such a lonely situation that I thought it should be avoided at all cost. And any type of sexual pleasure that might stand in the way of my dreams of attending college was simply out of the question. My mother made it crystal clear only my sister who was graduating from High school would be left in the house with her. My father, who had been sick his entire life had passed away the year before and my mother felt totally free of any type of shackles. My mother told my sister and I we could never leave anything that was alive with her. She told me, "I dreamed you would go to a big fancy college and that has been all you have ever talked about. But if you get pregnant, you better hope that school will supply room and board for you and that baby, because you will have that baby with you."

An unusual incident happened at the movies to my friend Janie who was about five years older than I. Some would even say it was a dangerous incident. Janie was always going to the movies by herself. One time she had to be brought home by her father. The Alfred Hitchcock movie "The Birds" scared Janie so much, she would not leave her seat until the usher called her home to have someone come get her. Janie's father, who had just gotten home from work, was very annoyed but went to pick her up. On the way home, he warned her never to go to the movies by herself. Of course, she paid no attention. She told me going alone to the movies made her feel like the star of a 1940's movie, all dressed up in a long-feathered gown, waiting for the man of her dreams to pick her up.

The theater was really empty, so Janie was a little surprised when a guy sat next to her. He was so fine she decided to keep her seat. All was going well. He said absolutely nothing to her, but she noticed he placed his left hand on the very edge of his seat. She wanted to be a sophisticated woman and not make a fuss, so she decided to keep her seat. He was so smooth, and as Janie said, so fine. He then gently let his left-hand rest upon her knee. He suddenly tongue kissed her and felt her up at the same time. Janie said he must have had an extra arm because it felt like his hands were all over her body and she believed she fainted. She must have been out for only a moment because when she came to she saw him running lighting fast toward the back of the movie theater. She could hardly believe her eyes when she caught a glimpse of him carrying her purse like a football tucked securely under his one arm while the other arm was extended straight out so as to push anyone out of his way. He was determined to get away with her purse. She wanted to scream "Stop him! He's got my purse!" But she remembered they had her dad's number and she had been warned about going to the theater alone. Janie decided her purse was payment for a lesson well learned. She figured it was the going price of a good kiss these days. And I thought, just maybe, there was hope for me because I truly learned from Janie's adventure.

Boyfriends & Other Situations

In the projects, seasonal abusive games were played by young boys throughout the year. Boys amused themselves with these games and over the course of time, they became quite skillful at tormenting the girls with spitballs, pea shooting paperclips, hair pulling, and throwing snowballs. Unfortunately, the only defense we girls had was to duck and dodge these assaults until these little negroes grew up. When these little boys became teenagers, they then developed a greater thirst to dominate women, and some would try and cop a feel uninvited. Can you blame me for being attracted to older boys? I had become weary at being shot at with all sorts of things by those imbeciles.

I wanted wider and greener pastures. It was time to spread my wings and meet older boys. I can now tell you; those greener pastures were sitting on cesspools. I entered the world of dating and life believing I knew everything. What I knew was absolutely nothing because I was speaking and trying to reason with the physical person. Proverbs 23:7 says, "As a man thinks in his heart so is he." So, trying to make your main man be a do right man is useless unless you have touched his heart. If not, he will just continue to blow smoke up your butt. I took these romantic betrayals quite hard because as I said, I knew everything. I thought a rational discussion with my man about his whorish behavior should have solved the problem. I soon realized these life situations came early to teach me a particularly challenging concept. That affairs of the heart are not usually settled with logic.

With that said, I became thoroughly impressed with my girlfriends' older brother Gerald. The first time I saw him a strange ache went through my stomach and somehow my panties got wet. Gerald's family lived on the first floor. I was in the lobby of the building speaking with Gerald's younger sister, and of course he paid me no attention as he stepped out into the winter's night. Oh, how I longed to enjoy a winter's night out with the man of my choice. A night with the snow lightly falling and the moon naturally creating a sliver grey haze with each falling snowflake that only an artist can dream of capturing on canvas. While imagining that sweet night, I could almost feel the lovely big fur collar coat all around my face. But alas, the streetlights had come on so my bewitching hour to go straight home had come and I was going to get into trouble because I was already late for my curfew. But before I got on to the elevator Gerald got my full attention. He walked right up to the front door without fear and yelled outside to those same cowardly boys who had just bullied me with the threat of being bombarded with snowballs. Gerald told them they had better hold up that snowball junk until he cleared the front door. In that New York minute, Gerald became my hero, but my heart would have to throb a bit longer until he broke his leg that summer.

Gerald had broken his leg playing basketball and was on crutches and unable to hang out with his regular friends. To escape cabin fever, Gerald decided to drop his elite status as one of the big boys and sit on the bench with those of us that were still unable to legally buy liquor. I was delighted with Gerald's present condition because he was now my constant companion. To my delight and amazement, Gerald was actually intelligent and quite witty. This was very surprising to me because remember, I knew everything. I was now his particular friend because he would call me in the morning to inform me of his day's itinerary and his attire. I was in seventh heaven to think a boy four years my senior was asking my opinion but being a man. Gerald also had that bragging defect when the conversation became boring. He naturally started glorifying his male genitalia because men think their male body parts are the great problem solvers of the free world. My first sexual experience was quite frightening. It started as all the summer days had been in the projects just hanging out on the bench waiting for someone to do something worth gossiping about.

There I was laughing and talking about current events of the day when Gerald decided to take the pink rubber tip off the top of his crutch and place it in an upright position between his thighs. While I was explaining the ways of the ghetto world, I glanced down and saw what I perceived to be his male body part out in the open for everyone's eyes to see. It scared me to the point that my feet took flight for about two blocks. I ran past all the older, yet young adults sitting in what we called the living room entrance of the projects. I hung right and went straight to main street, but I was still cooking. I ran one and a half city blocks. You have to understand. I was naive when it came to the male body. I had no brothers and had never seen an actual man's body. When I saw the pink tip of the crutch shaped like a huge sausage, I naturally jumped to the wrong conclusion. My girlfriend immediately realized it was only the top of Gerald's crutch because she had seen a penis on various occasions. I literally had to be shaken by the shoulders to bring me to my senses. My foolish mistake was enjoyed by many, but the revelation came to all of the boys my age and six years older. I was a unicorn. A fine genuine virgin in the ghetto with a fantastic shape and it was on and popping.

Gerald eventually healed from his leg injury and he now turned his full attention to getting me in bed. At a glance, I was unable to know the difference between a real penis and a piece of flesh-colored rubber shaped like a penis. But my sexual knowledge was quite clear about real penises and their ability to produce real babies. Having seen the number of baby carriages rolling around the projects in those days it was really apparent to me that these boys were working overtime making plenty of babies. These boys only wanted to rent those boxes. They NEVER intended to own a box and the very last thing these boys wanted were the little people that these boxes had a horrible habit of producing. I had never seen a college dorm room, but my aspirations knew how important I would be one day, and Gerald and those baby carriages had no part in my life.

My dream of going to college and being an independent career woman was working overtime in my mind. My favorite women on TV were the independent type. Gun Smoke's Miss Kitty who owned the LongBranch Saloon, Lieutenant Uhura of Star Track, and of course Lucille Ball of "I love Lucy" who was totally in charge of all those around her. With each exciting new day, my interest in Gerald started to disappear because there were so many more rewarding fish in my immediate sea. In my opinion, Gerald's personality was not strong enough to handle me or any of my TV women mentors. As a woman, I can connect a man to his dreams, but don't want to give him a desire to have dreams.

Soon God bailed me out and a young girl came along only wanting to escape her mother's house so a baby and a negro with a piece of job would do nicely. She and Gerald went off into the sunset for about a year and things went the way ghetto life does. He came back home to his mother's house and she moved into another project with a Department of Social Services budget of her own, but not before having another baby.

My friend Myra had an older brother getting married and when those types of things happen in the projects all family and friends got involved. It was tradition back in the day that a big wedding would mandate rehearsals for at least a full week in advance. This was usually just an excuse for a bunch of negros to get high and hang out until about eleven at night. The same party would restart the next night. Myra's brother was at least five years older than me and my main girl Janice, but Myra made sure we were a part of the gathering every night. This wedding came at an ideal time because my on and off again relationship with that no-good Jack, had left me with no one in my life. So, I jumped at a chance to be with someone I thought really had it going on. Janice and I met Myra's two cousins that were ushers in the wedding party. They lived in Queens but came every night to Brooklyn for the pre wedding festivities. I was interested in Carl and I genuinely loved the candy red Cadillac Eldorado he was driving. Carl was tall and slim with a fantastic smile. He was a light pecan tan with green eyes and he only seemed to be interested in little old me. Carl was such a gentleman. He made sure I had plenty to eat and drink and each time he rolled a joint it was as big as a cigarette. Let me tell you, I did look ghetto fabulous in that red Cadillac sitting next to Carl. I was the talk of the projects. All the girls wanted to know where this gorgeous fine brother came from and did I mention, his lovely red car was a convertible. My dream was complete. I always made sure to have Carl ride by where I knew Jack was sure to see me being wined and dined by Carl. Of course, Jack was right there at his house, because the cheap no-good son of a gun never took a woman out. He always entertained at his house because that way he spent no money. Whenever I rode by in that bad red Cadillac, Jack always acted as if he didn't see me riding with Carl, but I knew he did and the thrill it gave me was truly unbelievable. Unfortunately, Carl came every night with his cousin to the wedding rehearsal that week therefore, we never had any time alone. After we smoked and rode around, they both had jobs that required their early attention the next morning. To my dismay, Carl's cousin had an extremely early job schedule that he spoke about endlessly. By eleven o'clock they had to be on their merry way. No worries,

Janice and I looked forward and planned energetically for the wedding that Saturday. We both had our dresses made but due to my remarkable fashion sense, I helped with the designing of my outfit. We had the incredibly good fortune to live adjacent to a large Hasidic Jewish material district where they had the finest fabric that could rival the world market and those of Paris, France. Don't hear me say the bride did not look good, but I was divine. My dress was a tea-length Vogue pattern. It required minor alterations and showed off my hourglass shape and my flawless bareback. The material was a bright deep green vintage taffeta and it fit my body like a glove. When I stepped into the room, every man wanted my attention. After being there for about fifteen minutes, I became anxious because Carl was one of the ushers and he should have been there already. I decided to ask one of my acquaintances if she had seen Carl and his cousin. Before she could answer, Carl appeared out of nowhere and kissed me right on the lips. Immediately a woman snatches him from my embrace and slaps him so hard I felt the vibration off her hand. As quick as a flash she stepped toward me, but I pushed Carl in front of her and she slapped the mess out of him again. Now it was on! This time he retaliated and grabbed her hands and they then hit the floor. Even though there was an entire room full of confusion, I could clearly hear Carl's wife say, "I am going to kick that husband stealing heifer's behind right now."

Janice and I made a mad dash to the door and we didn't stop running until we entered Janice's front door. Needless to say, I was sadly disappointed and very embarrassed. I could still hear the laughter ringing in my head. I have no idea what I looked like trying to make my escape in that very tight dress. I just thank my lucky stars I begged my mother to put such a high split in that dress. Otherwise, I would have needed to pull that dress way up over my behind to get the type of speed I needed to leave that place. I never heard from Carl again after that horrible episode. Once I gained enough composure to confer with Myra, I found out the she-devil was Carl's wife of six years. Myra said because her cousins lived in Queens, she knew little about their marriage status. I later found out Carl's wife was famous for fighting women when it concerned husband. Lord, I was glad to have gotten away from her without having gotten my behind kicked that night.

So, I positively, absolutely was not going to date Gerald, and I surely wasn't going to risk getting beat up by Carl's hellcat of a wife. But I soon left the kettle and jumped right on to the piping hot stove. Jack was back and I was truly out of my league. He was six years my senior, with a girlfriend attached to his side, that seven years his senior. But remember, I knew everything. As those foreign customer service people always say, "no worries."

I fell crazy in love with a man in a "Drum and bugle corps" uniform. To tell you the truth, this man had the same heart for me as a nutcracker soldier toy. He was tall, with a light pecan tan complexion and I wish I could say he was handsome. But that would be a lie straight from the pits of hell from which he came. The problem was he had huge lips, small slits for eyes, and a little head. Jack was so much older than I so we both knew my mother was going to present a problem. So, for many years, I hid my relationship with him from my family and my mother's close friends. Little did I know, this was exactly what Jack wanted. He wanted to keep our relationship as secret as possible. Once I graduated from high school Jack finally got the nerve to come to my house and I was not home at the time. My mother could have dropped to the floor. My mother later told me Jack was never to return to our house because she didn't want any of her friends to see him. She said he was way too old for me and his lips were so large he resembled a clown with a permanent ridiculous smile on his face. Don't hear me say my mother was wrong about his age, or the size and look of his lips. But my mother could not have guessed the magic power those lips had on me. Jack's lips were way ahead of their time. They seemed to be made out of lush memory foam that kissed me so wonderfully I said Hallelujah.

I was in love with that clown and would have run away and married him at the drop of a hat. The problem was Jacky the clown was not running away with jailbait or anyone else because he was living a charmed life. He had a string of women that simply adored him. All his other women were of age, and to my knowledge, I was the only 14-year-old in the pack he was sneaking around with. To add to my troubles, his main woman Clara was working, paying bills, administering his political headquarters, and running the home front. Jack ran around with women and dabbled in politics as much as his money could afford him and was looking forward to one day becoming a city councilman. As far as I knew, he was always at the grassroots level of the political game but never made any real money. He was not successful because in the very beginning of your political career you have to display a real heart for the people you will serve, and Jack wasn't that person. I would later find out he had a stingy selfish nature that even extended towards his mother. The Bible says, you reap what you sow, and my rule is to avoid any man that is unfair to his mother.

Now, I must admit Jack had it going on. He had a charismatic personality and big dreams about politics. This combination kept my foolish head right up in his behind. Me and Jack's romance was a constant on and off thing due to all his other women and his "play-play" political career. Jack and I had the gift of being very witty, and we enjoyed much laughter until I simply forgot how horrible he treated me. Subsequently, I learned to overlook his flaws which were many. I know God structured his face, so I suppose he wasn't able to control his ridiculous expressions and big lips. But from experience, I can tell you that being an ugly child can give you a warped personality as an adult if you never overcome the stigma of your looks. A powerful ugly man can be hell, because he is always trying to overcome his past hurts. You had better be strong and confident in your love for yourself otherwise, he will eat you alive. The flip side of this coin is that extremely handsome men are used to having their way with little effort. They will walk on you until they grow tired and then throw you out with the trash. Jack was a notorious whore. His deceitfulness was unbounded. He was a self-centered, stingy bastard that only took me to the movies once in our entire courtship. I guess some of those traits were perfect for today's politicians. Even though I was deeply in love with Jack, I never allowed my goal of going away to college to get away from me and cause me to blunder into indulging in a physically penetrating sexual relationship at an early age. When Jack and I finally went to bed, I was about twenty-one. I had all sorts of beautiful fantasies about how our first time was going to be. I had dreamed about that moment for many years. Even with my inexperience, I knew Jack was horrible and only cared about himself. The strange and frightening thing about the human psyche is we can accept so many flaws in our chosen mate. In the animal kingdom, they would have seen those flaws as a deal-breaker and would have moved on to a more suitable mate. Looking back, I now know Jack was a selfish person in and out of the bedroom and that I should have run away from him long ago.

Jack kept a large amount of marijuana, he loved being around people, he enjoyed music, and he was a personable party host. These were the best things about him, and they kept our relationship going. So, my advice to him if he was going to succeed in politics, was for him to continue to be his lying, dishonest yet charismatic self but to always keep the music playing and the party going.

I had such an early curfew during my teen years I never got to fully enjoy Jack's parties. There were always lots of people around Jack's house in the afternoon, so we had little alone time and few make-out opportunities. Unfortunately, with so many people around hardcore petting was also out of the question which was the one thing Jack was extremely good at.

Jack and his main woman Clara taught me many lessons over the years. I don't know how Jack arranged it, but Clara did not always stay at Jack's house. Jack won the daily double when he got Clara. She was smart enough to hold a good job but so naïve as to be a complete doormat for him in every way. He somehow convinced her to take on quite a few of the financial responsibilities at his home even though she did not own or reside there full time. Jack was exceptionally shrewd and lucky at manipulating Clara into paying for all his political adventures that flopped. She was a true believer in the ridiculous dreams that he didn't really want to work at achieving. George Koufalis wrote a book titled, "The Dream is free, but the hustle is sold separately." And I can tell you Jack was definitely not hustling. In addition, someone who is deliberately creating bad karma will never have a truly successful destiny. That's just the way of the world and I should not have wanted to be part of such a person's scheme. Jack could always count on Clara's donations to pay for guest speakers', musical equipment, and renting clubs for gala events. But even with his love and know-how for the political world and all the donations he acquired from Clara and others, Jack never reached the stardom he was seeking. I learned early I too would pay for my secondary part in this whole ugly love triangle. My strips were to have a lifetime of unreasonable suspicion when it came to my mate. When you willingly play a part, no matter how minor in hurting someone, you invite that same spirit to hover over your life. So, be careful in all situations you involve yourself in, because I learned some grownup lessons about men and women's relationships early in my young teenage life.

Whenever Jack had parties, he would have both Clara and I there. Due to my curfew, I was never able to wait her out. I usually saw Jack during the day and early evening while Clara was at work. Once, Jack seemed to be getting serious about another girl named Sally and she was cutting into my daytime visits. I got the bright idea I should meet Clara at the bar she went to after work and let her know about Sally. I went to the bar straight after school, so I got there quite a while before Clara arrived. By the time Clara got there, some older men had been buying me drinks. I had never drunk before so when these older guys offered me a drink, I ordered what I saw my mother drink. They were all quite amused that my drink of choice was Johnny Walker Black with a club soda back. After one drink, I wasn't feeling too good, so I ducked into the bathroom and took a few hits off a joint and the world calmed down again. When Clara got there, I must have talked a little too much and she became furious. During the argument, Clara alluded to the fact I was only fourteen years old. She also told me I had a lot of nerve sitting up there on a damn bar stool in my school uniform telling her about her fiancée. I was extremely fortunate she did not kick my butt right then and there on the spot. Actually, it was the owner of the bar that actually saved my behind because he didn't want any trouble with a minor at his bar. He put me in a cab and sent me home. After that, I avoided Clara like the plague. When I thought about it afterwards, how did those men never see my school uniform until Clara called it to their attention? That was the day I realized men think with the heads in their pants and not with the head on their shoulders. I had narrowly escaped getting a good behind cutting and Clara must have also taken care of Sally because I never saw her again.

I allowed Jack's lies to lull me into those always happy endings of the ever so popular sitcoms of the day. I had the romantic notion that the sweet girl always eventually gets the boy, and they lived happily ever after. Good lord was I ever wrong. Older women who have earned their big girl cotton panties would have realized just how much foolishness Jack was slinging and I caught it all. Jack always had numerous extenuating circumstances that I allowed him to spoon-feed me why we were unable to function as real a couple, and I ate his lies up like chocolate kisses. This is how Jack's story went. First, Jack told me he loved me best, and the only reason he kept Clara around was to pay the bills. Jack said since I was his girlfriend and whenever he slept, he banished himself to the couch. Do you believe I actually went for such foolishness? But I do know women right now that go for the same silly story. He then went on to tell me it was my mother who was the one keeping us apart because of my age. Granted, she was, but how convenient for him. To tell the truth, my mother wasn't even aware of my great love affair because Jack and I kept us on the downlow. Jack said, "I have very little time for our relationship because my real energy has to be spent pursuing a political career and leading people to a righteous life." Of course, I believed him. He always worked at making me think he and his whole family intensely disliked Clara and loved me best. Of course, old lady time and her girlfriend twenty-twenty hindsight had quite a different scenario ending for my torrid love affair with Jack. When Jack was finally forced to decide, he chose Clara and rightfully so. I was just an outside woman who was young and misinformed. He and his entire family, who had told me they really loved me best, embraced Clara with open arms like I never existed. When I tearfully related the entire sorted story to my mother, she had two very loving and valuable pieces of advice for me. She said, "It is extremely hard to take a man away from his wife." And of course, that I should leave that situation alone. My mother said something else important that I always want you to remember, "Everyone loves a winner." And as we know, Clara won. As Crosby Stills and Nash said, "Teach your children well."

Girls, Girls, Girls

My friends and I allowed Motown to teach us about love affairs, family matters, and life in general. Mr. Right was only a kiss away and this fantasy had no age limit. Old and young women alike were foolishly caught up in this trap. We refused to take the Spinners seriously when they explicitly told us "That love don't love nobody." Instead, we listened to Diana Ross when she said, "Someday we'll be together" and we trusted that like money in the bank.

Motown had us all in a magical world of love. Men loved women hard and strong therefore we believed what Mr. Otis Redding said. Every woman over the age of thirty was madly in love with Otis. He was a man's man. Even if he were not your particular type physically his words made you know that he could make it right. If your husband was dead or you had a no-good boyfriend who wasn't doing his job, Otis was "Loving you too long to stop now." Which was something every woman wanted to hear. So, the saying goes, a man will ask a woman do you love me? A woman will always ask a man do you STILL love me? When

Otis' death was announced my mother and her friends cried as if the love of their life had passed. During the Motown era, Black women started thinking about White men differently. A Black woman could freely dream romantically about a White man, such as Sean Connery James Bond 007 he was no longer exclusively for a White woman.

Cherie came that summer to babysit her Aunt Mabel's two daughters. She loved project life so much she never went back home. Cherie was about four years older than all the girls in the building but since she had to stay home and babysit her nieces every day, we were the only game in town. Cherie had eleven siblings and the only advise her mother gave her as she departed was "After sex, pee as hard as you can and that will stop you from getting pregnant." Cherie was sixteen and I was thirteen when she gave me that advice. But knowing Cherie's mother had twelve children, it just didn't seem like something I wanted to count on. Her Aunt Mabel wasn't going to count on it either. She considered her sister's birth control advice to be absolutely positively ridiculous. Cherie arrived on a Saturday and come Monday Aunt Mabel had Cherie at the free birth control clinic. Aunt Mabel had a very demanding job and a husband that ran around quite frequently depositing his money at hairy banks. So, she had little time to monitor Cherie's sexual activities. Aunt

Mabel had all the children she wanted and by no means did she bring Cherie there to populate her home.

Immediately, Cherie showed all of us what the birth control clinic had given her and she also shared her advice about taking birth control. We gave Cherie our undivided attention because no one wanted to miss any juicy details about these wonder drugs and tools that were going to allow us to be independent women. We had never seen these types of trinkets before, so Cherie allowed each of us to touch the trojans. The real thrill came when we touched the diaphragm. It looked like a sink stopper turned upside down, but we knew it had nothing to do with washing dishes! Cherie even demonstrated how it was installed. Now, you have to know this was really exciting for us because while we all had our periods, none of us had even used a tampon before. The clinic had given Cherie an assortment of birth control and instructions on how to use them. She was ready, and so this boy crazy thing she was feeling was going to work out just fine. Cherie already knew her way around the bedroom before she came to the projects. But now, she had sound advice on how to avoid getting pregnant.

Cherie was light skinned with an angelic face and a body that looked like it had been carved from the Greek sex goddess Aphrodite. Cherie knew she had a great shape, and now that she was armed with birth control, her goal was to show her great shape to every man who had eyes. A man never had to put Cherie on a "layaway plan." He was guaranteed to get her into bed because she obeyed the words of the Isely Brothers, "Love the one you're with." Cherie quickly became the most popular girl in the neighborhood. Her popularity exploded so much Aunt Mabel sent for Cherie's mother in the hope that she could reprimand her daughter about her whorish ways. Unfortunately, that mother-daughter talk was to no avail and Cherie just went underground with her sexual activities.

Cherie was our girl and all, but she had a way of thinking we were not familiar with and a disease we were way too young to realize. Cherie was suffering from a sex addiction. None of us had even had "sex" that involved someone else. The only addictive behaviors we were familiar with were drugs and alcohol addiction. Unfortunately, the adults in charge of Cherie's upbringing had no understanding of sex addiction either. So instead of getting her the help she desperately needed to correct the unhealthy behavior, they labeled her a "fast behind" girl. Once Cherie became older, people in the projects said she was a woman with a "White liver." It wasn't until much later I learned the term "White liver" referred to a very promiscuous woman that had an insatiable urge to have sex whenever, and wherever she wanted. That description fit Cherie's everyday activity because she was having sex with whoever at least three times a day whenever possible.

Cherie went on to graduate from high school and became a health care worker at a neighboring hospital. Life for Cherie moved on and she eventually married a military man. She had a good life, but she couldn't keep her "fast behind '' satisfied with man. Last I heard, HIV had the final say and Cherie passed away during the Aids pandemic.

My friends and I were inspired when Motown said, "You can't hurry love, no, you just have to wait…no matter how long it takes." And rest assured we were willing to wait a long time for that perfect life. We trusted and believed in Motown because it seemed they were the only ones who believed in us. We saw three girls, from the housing projects of Detroit, become big stars like the Beatles and be televised on the Ed Sullivan Show which was the hottest TV show in town during that time. Motown showed us there was more to life for Black women than cooking and cleaning in some White woman's home. We might have come from the projects, but our beautiful black skin was not going to hold us back and keep us there.

Unfortunately, during the Motown era, there were families in the projects that lived like my friend Suzanne. Suzanne and her family were totally dysfunctional. They seemed to live life like they had gum stuck on the bottom of both shoes. Suzanne and her three sisters lived in an impoverished alcoholic environment. Their mother had a disease and they also had an extremely abusive father that paid them no attention. Suzanne and her sisters were constantly being physically and emotionally hurt because they had no support at home and their peers had not yet developed the ability to nurture them. Suzanne couldn't understand why their peers wouldn't open their hearts and share what they had with her and her sisters. These poor girls had no way of realizing how formattable the foe was that competed with them for their peer's charitable attention. As we have all come to learn, television is a relentless teacher, and the lessons are hard and simple. Those that are weak, and poor will be crushed as America marches on. The American theme of every man having his own was already strongly embedded in the minds of most young teens. By Junior high school, I was already in competition to confirm to the world I was living my best life. This attitude prevented me from readily extending any of my physical or spiritual props in a kind and helping way to Suzanne. I can only imagine the shame of constantly borrowing and having to accept handouts that came from a resentful giver. This type of shame would never have allowed these girls to know the queen inside of them that so desperately wanted to live. Not knowing their worth, Suzanne and her sisters followed the unfortunate, yet common ghetto life cycle, taking life's leftovers of institutionalized living, early death, and worst of all a life of hopelessness. My Lord in heaven please help us.

Suzanne inherited her mother's great looks. She had long, thick, brown hair and her skin was the color of a gold autumn leaf. She had an hourglass shape with an ample behind and her facial features closely resembled an Italian beauty. However, her common sense played hide-and-seek with her, and ruthlessly won every game. We girls could have shared more of our clothes with her but being young and still looking for our place in the spotlight of life we were not as charitable as we should have been. Suzanne had another problem when it came to borrowing our clothes, she never returned them and when she did return our belongings, they were barely recognizable. For example, Suzanne would return a pair of socks she said were washed and they felt like they could have stood up and walked back to you on their own. So, therefore, we grudgingly shared with her a few of our least liked clothing items. But the few clothes we did give up she made them look fabulous because she was simply gorgeous. Suzanne never allowed the burden of her alcoholic mother, the indifference of her father, or her three needy younger sisters to get her into a depressed state. I don't know if she was just too dumb to realize life had dealt her a bleak hand or did she purposely avoid taking a good look. Suzanne must have realized early in life her good looks were her only asset at having the good life those Motown songs had promised because academics was not her strong suit. Regrettably, there was no adult in her life that cared about her education or cared enough to encourage her to succeed in life. Suzanne was never able to pull herself out of the grave dilemma she was experiencing at home and sadly, she never graduated Junior High School.

All of us girls dressed alike every Saturday and went to matinee rock'n'roll shows that featured incredible talent but cost only a dollar. After the show, we always went to Suzanne's Aunt Jenny's house where we danced and sang our hearts out to Motown songs in our short, pleated skirts. We loved it! Aunt Jenny was the closest person to ghetto rich that we knew, and her house was ghetto fabulous. Most importantly, we all got to call her aunt Jenny and she treated us like family. Aunt Jenny had two grown sons that were hardcore convicts with real rough life histories that they unfortunately never used as learning experiences. But neither one of them ever made any sexual advances towards us. These men treated us like the daughters they never had. They always bought us lots of fast food and Jenny baked cakes and pies that we ate until we were stuffed. Suzanne's aunt Jenny was the one bright light that she had in her otherwise stomach-turning life. Aunt Jenny was Suzann's mother's sister and she never drank or indulged in low life living. Aunt Jenny knew her worth and didn't allow her husband to take her for granted or at least where she would notice.

Aunt Jenny only worked a few days a week because she wanted something to do while her husband Ben was away driving his long-haul tractor trailer. All the girls loved and dreamed about having Aunt Jenny's house because it was a fine place to live. Aunt Jenny used to be a live-in maid for extraordinarily rich people and had been around the finer things in life and knew what was possible for her beautiful niece. Aunt Jenny did have some regrets. As a live-in maid she had very little time for her children. Aunt Jenny allowed her past poverty to persuade her to chase a lustful promise of money and neglected her first responsibility which was raising her children. When children are left to themselves exclusively there are going to be serious problems. Her oldest son spent ten years in jail and her youngest son did a seven-year jail sentence.

Now that Aunt Jenny had time, she was seeking the redemption of her past mistakes with her niece Suzanne. Aunt Jenny felt in her heart of hearts she could correct Suzanne's life. Aunt Jenny tried to encourage Suzanne in all types of ways to come and live with her but once a child has gotten used to living as they pleased voluntary submission is next to impossible. The Book of Revelation 3:17 (New International Version) says, "You say, 'I am rich; I have acquired wealth and do not need a thing.' But you do not realize that you are wretched, pitiful, poor, blind and naked." I believe Suzanne might have allowed her Aunt Jenny to help her more, but a few things were holding her back. First, Suzanne's laziness kept her bound to where she was. She would rather take the hand-me-downs of others rather than live a comfortable life with simple rules and a solid foundation. Second, Suzanne knew her mother Eva knew Aunt Jenny's husband Ben in the biblical sense and met him once a week for fifteen lousy dollars. Ben used Suzanne's mother, his sister-in-law, Miss Eva, sexually once a week in the bed of his tractor-trailer for pennies. I've seen those who have no morals and practice an unscrupulous life and even sometimes good and ordinary people who are unable to resist temptation do dirty unfair things to the pitiful. A woman suffering from the disease of alcohol addiction trying to make ends meet for her habit and maybe a pair of shoes for a child is bound to do shameful acts. So, you see Suzanne's life was very complicated for such a young girl of thirteen years old.

Uncle Ben, who was married to Aunt Jenny, was Ghetto rich. He made an excellent salary for a black man during that time. There were many legal and illegal perks for a trucker and his family to enjoy before the age of computers came about to keep an accurate account of the inventory hauled and company financials. In the 1960's a Black man who earned a large salary legally was a rare bird and a lot of these men used poor Black women to satisfy their sexual appetites to the fullest. Financially well-off Black men that cheated did a lot of sneaking around with poor women who were trying to supplement their household income. These women usually made the mistake of thinking these affairs were real love and had children outside of their homes. Mother Nature can be tricky extramarital sex can be real HOT causing a disruption in a woman's ovulation schedule boom there a baby. Now, her husband knows this child is not his blood, but he is aware of all the ends being met in their household because of this other man. Her husband can conclude his wife is just a whore or he comes to terms with the gut-wrenching pain that his inability to supply the basic needs for their family has demanded this type of behavior from his wife. I guess it comes down to which of the two evils you can stomach. Living with the guilt of abandoning your family, or can you tolerate your wife and her outside child. You better believe this still goes on to this very day.

With no parental direction, Suzanne never walked towards the light. Her Aunt Jenny was devastated with how Suzanne's life ended. Suzanne became involved with heroin at the age of fifteen and by nineteen she had two children. Suzanne soon gravitated towards the heroin addicts Mecca, which at that time was Harlem, NY. There, she met a poor excuse for a pimp who was 52 years old and reminded you of a high yellow, blue-eyed Leprechaun and with the personality of a chump. In the rough world of turning tricks and drug addiction, I seriously don't know how effective he could have been as a pimp. They would come and spend a few days at Suzanne's mother's house and run some sucker games on slow dimwit heroin addicts in the project. Everything about this little Leprechaun pimp Suzanne had was impoverished. A pimp without a car, a roof over his head and who was a frequent flyer at the Department of Welfare is seriously a poor excuse for a pimp. A month after meeting him, Suzanne was pregnant with her third child and how profitable could that have been. I always thought pimps wanted their hired whores to be shapely so they would produce as much cash as possible. Only in the world of the horse (heroin) could you pimp a nine-month pregnant woman to produce a sufficient amount of money to support his and her heroin habit. I honestly think the little leprechaun saw Suzanne two ways. First, as his sexual money maker and second, as the mother of his children. Some said Suzanne ran a game on her pimp and her third baby was not his, but that was a lie. That baby was a tiny blue-eyed replica= of his Leprechaun father. Just before her twenty-first birthday, Suzanne passed away from hepatitis. "When I'm gone" by Mary Wells was Suzanne's favorite Motown song. Suzanne never quite understood why people were never as loving towards her as she was with them. I guess her theme song should have been "Ghetto Child."

The Anderson family was more like a clan than other families. The mother had the confidence of Michelle Obama but the looks and sex appeal of R2 D2, but this defect never stopped her from getting the man she wanted to marry. Mrs. Anderson was five feet, four inches tall and she weighed about one hundred and thirty pounds. She was shaped like an ice cream cone because she had absolutely no behind but wore a very large bra size of 34DD. Maybe it was those big pecan breasts and that fifth of liquor that kept Mr. Anderson home every night. Mrs. Anderson had short, measly hair that she barely kept done. Her dental hygiene was awful to say the least, and she had large brown crooked teeth. After years of drinking alcohol, I guess the sugar started to rot her teeth. Mr. Anderson was at one time a very handsome man until alcohol wreaked havoc on his looks and eventually his health. Mr. Anderson was about six feet, two inches tall with very fair skin and straight loosely curly brown hair. When I met Mr. and Mrs. Anderson, they were both on the decline, but I am sure of one thing, Mrs. Anderson and those three ordinary-looking girls were nothing to write home about and Mrs. Anderson somehow hoodwinked him into a marriage. I think Mr. Anderson started drinking at a very young age and what Mrs. Anderson pulled off with that marriage was truly a stroke of luck with his brain being pickled in alcohol. I believe my mother was jealous of Mrs. Anderson because she always said, Mrs. Anderson was a good for nothing chick that never had to work a day in her life. My mother went on to say that Mrs. Anderson must have possessed a box with black magic love making ability because there was no way an alcoholic nasy housekeeping woman could catch a hardworking good man like Mr. Anderson. Mrs. Anderson always had words of what she called wisdom for her daughters and any of the other girls who would listen. She always told us girls, "Some women can go to the moon and make ice cream, and then some confused cows cannot find a rock on the beach." She said, you have to decide early in life what type of woman you want to be because that body will not be young forever. After all, it is hard to change horses in the middle of the road with an old, dry, non-inviting body.

Mrs. Anderson had four children and out of the four only the youngest, a boy was Mr. Anderson's by blood. Neither one of them were strict disciplinarians so with such a loose hold over the children, they were allowed to do as they pleased. I think everybody in the building was amazed that all the kids graduated from school. The oldest girl Tina graduated from high school with a practical nursing degree even though she got pregnant in her last year of high school, and then backed it up with a second baby because I guess the first one was such fun. The other girls' Kat and Marjorie came right out of high school and got good jobs and the baby boy James graduated from high school and became a notorious but really successful drug dealer that somehow never went to jail. None of the children had an appetite for the bottle praise God.

Mainly, Mrs. Anderson was never going to allow the children to stay home and annoy her beauty rest during the day. So, they had to go somewhere, and I guess it was just easier for them to go to school than find someplace to hang out. Mrs. Anderson did not play with you when it came to disrespecting your elders, so the children gave their teachers no problem in that area. Whenever our girlfriends in the building wanted to compare a place to a pigsty, we would always use the Anderson's as our go-to reference for uncleanliness. It was an ongoing joke amongst us that the piles of clothes they kept on the floor that reached to the ceiling was the home for a family of mice. The only thing I think they didn't have on the kitchen counters was rotten food but every darn thing else in the free world was in that kitchen. Mrs.

Anderson had ample money and a genuine love for fine beautiful things, but it was her affliction of laziness that kept her home in such shambles. Even as a teenager I loved Mrs. Anderson's sets of exquisite deep-colored thick glass dishes which were dark green and red. She had groceries everywhere and those beautiful dishes were mixed right in that squalor. Mrs. Anderson always invited you to eat, and she would serve you food on those good dishes because she never waited for a special occasion. Her motto was to eat, drink and enjoy for tomorrow was not a promise to anyone. We girls would go there occasionally but we just preferred to go to each other's houses and stay out of that pigpen. Suzanne went there all the time because she and her sister had very little food and the Anderson's were a hospitable family that was always cooking food, eating, and drinking.

I never remember Mrs. Anderson cheating on her husband, and she would have had plenty of opportunities because her husband was either at work or out cold drunk in the bed. The Andersons could have reminded you of Suzanne's family because of alcoholism but they had money to buy all the things they wanted. Mr. Anderson worked every day at a well-paying city job. Before the internet, any self-respecting ghetto queen, and Mrs. Anderson surely was an old, smart ghetto queen, because she always had at least three people in her family who qualified for help from the state. With the three that qualified for a check, there was always a real party going on day and night. Tina was the oldest sister, and she took us all out with her to the discos where her boyfriend was a bartender. We could drink all we wanted to for the entire night. None of the girls in the building were big drinkers so our parents never objected. Tina thought she would make some extra money by helping girls terminate their pregnancy. Before Roe v. Wade abortions were illegal and there was real money to be made if you knew how to perform an illegal abortion. That was not my thing. I didn't need an abortion, nor was I interested in performing one.

Alice was one of our friends that was not in our main circle because she did not hang out with us most of the time and she already had a baby. Alice and I were both fifteen, but she seemed so much older than me in a hardcore way. Maybe it was having a baby at thirteen that started her into dating much older men. I got the impression Alice was turning tricks because of the large amounts of money she always had whenever we hung out together and her expensive clothes were endless. My mother was working the late night third shift these days so when Alice invited me to a party I was overjoyed. Alice only went to grownup sophisticated parties and that meant it would be lots of interesting people and plenty of marijuana. Alice hailed a cab, and we went up to 96th street in Manhattan and the cab cost way more money than I had to spend. The party was fabulous, the food was super, and Alice introduced me to a guy, but he was old enough to be my grandfather. I told her I was not interested, and she put me back in a cab, shoved eighty dollars in my hand and slammed the door. Alice found herself pregnant again at fifteen and birth control pills were already legal, so I don't know what was her story? Did Alice think one of those rich old men was going to marry her? Women can make serious errors when they make important decisions that hinge on living by the exceptions to the rule.

I really don't know what her train of thought was when she allowed Tina and her friend to perform an abortion that nearly cost her to lose her life. Maybe it was because she lived with an older cousin who she didn't have to answer to so therefore she lived her life as she wanted, maybe it was a money thing because I don't think there are too many pregnant escorts being requested in large numbers, and maybe she panicked because her first baby had taken so much of her youthful freedom and the thought of having another baby was too much for her to handle. But let me tell you, Alice didn't take a chance with Tina and her friend, what she took was a suicide mission because they were a butchering crew. I always believed a lot of healthy women of childbearing age during that time, died suddenly because of illegal abortions. I understand Tina led that ghastly operation and her medical experience was limited because she was a practical nurse who worked in a nursing home. I don't know what made her think she was qualified to discharge that baby away from Alice's uterus. Anyway, as the story goes, they had to hide this covert operation from Mrs. Anderson. Even though she was drunk most of the time, Mrs. Anderson was as sharp as a switchblade. Their little adventure started on a Friday night, and they had a minor setback which turned into a major situation. Alice's uterus did not readily release the fetus and Tina and her accomplice were too afraid to call 911. If you can believe it, Alice didn't want them to call either even though she was in a great amount of pain and was running a very high fever. All of this would have been enough for me. I don't know if it was her pride or shame that kept her in that room at death's door?

That Saturday morning, all of us girls were going ice skating at Prospect park. After skating we decided to go to Aunt Jenny's house. Kat and Marjorie broke down crying hysterically and told us the secret they had held as long as they could. They both thought Alice was going to die, and their sister Tina would go to Jail. When they told us about Alice and the botched abortion, we could hardly believe it. We were just there that morning, picking them up from their house while Alice was lying there dying on the other side of the door. Suzanne immediately told

Aunt Jenny and she told Kat and Marjorie to call their mother immediately! When Kat & Marjorie called home, their Sister Tina said their mother was talking to the Ambulance driver. Tina had already confessed most of the story to her mother about Alice being in the bedroom probably dying from an incomplete abortion that she had tried to perform Friday night. After a short while Aunt Jenny got the full report from Mrs. Anderson on what happened with Alice. Mrs. Anderson said she heard Alice screaming in pain and of course it woke her up. She went to see what was going on and saw that Alice was hemorrhaging profusely. Her daughter Tina told her what happened, and while she was furious with all of them she composed herself and immediately called 911.

Since abortion was illegal during this time and carried a heavy stigma, Alice didn't want to admit to the doctors what had happened. Miss Anderson, who went to the hospital with Alice witnessed her perform a drawn-out, overly dramatic skit begging the doctors to save her baby. The doctors told Alice that was impossible, and they would have to perform a dilate and curettage to remove the remaining tissue from her uterus. In other words, they had to perform a D&C to save her life. Since abortion wasn't legal at this time, I'm sure the hospital staff saved many a patient with the same story and performance as Alice. After a day or two when Alice's fever had gone down, and she was clear of any infection they let her go home and no one went to Jail.

However, Miss Anderson was on the war path and she cussed her daughter Tina out every time she laid eyes on her. She wanted to know who else was in on this ridiculously dangerous scheme that could have caused their family to be put out of the Marcy Projects and might have very well killed Alice. Miss Anderson just couldn't believe her daughter Tina, who she thought was the smartest of her children, would have done such a stupid thing as trying to give someone an abortion. From then on, Miss Anderson called Tina dumb Dr. Casy until Tina moved out of the project's years later.

Miss Evelyn

(Only Doing What They Understood)

Miss Evelyn was dealt a rough hand of cards she had to play her entire life. She might have gotten a new hand, but never a winning hand. Evelyn's genealogy was American Indian, and Irish Caucasian once removed. She had inherited her grandfather's strong White genes and her family had a lot of White traits that stirred up trouble within their Black community. This envy was earnestly felt because in the White man's eyes, the traits of Evelyn's family were more tolerable. Because of these White traits, Evelyn's family received more opportunities for financial gain. Darker Blacks hated that White people held "high yellow" Negroes in higher esteem. A Black woman with White features was deemed to be pretty by White men's standards and this caused problems for White and Black women. All of the women in Evelyn's family had fair mulatto skin. Some could even pass for White with their long silky hair requiring no straightening comb. Another peculiar point about

Evelyn's family was their love and devotion to attaining education and this habit continues to this very day. Miss Evelyn's mother and father's whole generation could read and write and this love for education would produce a large number of college graduates even though they were a small family. In the 1930's, 40's and 50's Evelyn's family had fewer financial burdens than many Blacks during that time so they could concentrate on the finer things of life such as education.

Miss Evelyn grew up in a small southern town which was the central location for rural shoppers. Her family, the McCabe's were considered well to do but would have been considered quite poor in this new day of food stamps, welfare, and the internet. Beth, Miss Evelyn's mother had done a terrible thing at the young age of thirteen by getting pregnant. This immoral act of Miss Beth's caused Evelyn to be born under a cloud of shame. It was a disgrace that rocked the entire family. Evelyn's father Norman was a few years older than her mother Miss Beth. Maybe that's why he was able to persuade her to go against everything her family taught. Norman was Beth's first love. She saw her life in his eyes, and he thought Miss Beth had the aroma of sweet potatoes with pure vanilla. But he also got a whiff of stench from the sweat and manure that came from his long day of pushing a wretched plow. Norman began to realize Miss Beth's sweet body was talking to his body way louder than his heartfelt dreams were now able to speak. Norman's dreams of keeping the dust off of his shiny shoes and a croaker sack off his back were starting to become hazy. Miss Beth was whispering in Norman's ear and her lovemaking was carrying a big stick. It was whipping the heck out of Norman's dreams. But what frightened Norman most about Miss Beth was the fact that she was unaware of the strong spiritual love for hard country living she carried in her heart. Norman told Miss Beth repeatedly he would be an important man in life. He felt some men were mules and other men were made to ride mules. So, in the end, Norman's passion for a tuxedo lifestyle and his vow to never again have a mule fart in his face drove him straight to the big city of New York where he remained for the rest of his life. Norman never again allowed a pretty woman to slow him up from his dream of becoming an important rich man.

Because Norman abandoned Miss Beth publicly, her suffering went way beyond just getting pregnant without a husband. She also carried the shame of being made a complete fool. This type of misstep did not happen to the women in Miss Beth's family. They were careful that nothing was done in the open where society could take notice. The McCabe family was considered well to do who had good girls that later would become teachers and nurses. This type of embarrassment only happened to lower-class dark skin girls or so the McCabe's would have you believe. Norman betrayed Beth in the worst way a man could. He deceived a woman he professed his love for and then left her without a trace. The only evidence Miss Beth had of him ever being there was the baby he left in her belly. Because of Miss Beth's situation, every female in her family was now looked upon differently, like they too might be easily manipulated. Deception has such a lasting effect. It leaves a person doubting every future decision they make and as far as men were concerned Miss Beth would never get it right.

Miss Beth got married young and it was a very foolish thing to do but she had to get away from her father's disappointed eyes and his constant belittling remarks that cut like a knife. Miss Beth getting pregnant brought disgrace to their good name and this event had the entire family in turmoil. Miss Beth did her very best to avoid her father's company. She even tried to stay at her aunt's house but Mr. McCabe being old, set in his ways, and a lay preacher said she was not to take her shame to other family members. Therefore, Miss Beth had to live at home. This harassment would go on every day for hours at a time until her father finally went to bed. Now, once Miss Evelyn was born, Mr. McCabe loved and adored her even more than his own children, but he still continued to harass Miss Beth making her life absolutely miserable. When Miss Evelyn was about six months old, Miss Beth fell in love with Mr. Melvin. Mr. Melvin was a hard-working Lumberjack that was willing to take Miss Beth and baby Evelyn into his home. Miss Beth was blindly in love with Mr. Melvin, but he turned out to be an extremely jealous man and a notorious whore around town. Miss Beth did her best to ignore Mr. Melvin's running around. He was after all a hardworking man that paid the bills. When Evelyn was about twelve, Mr. Melvin took a job 100 miles away and commuted home every weekend. Mr. Melvin got involved with some woman and didn't return for two months. Miss Beth became desperate and had someone send a telegram to Mr. Melvin's job that she had passed away. This shocking news brought Melvin home that very day. Once Mr. Melvin arrived at the house, there sat Miss Beth laughing and talking with her sisters and neighbors. Mr. Melvin was furious and the only reason he didn't jump on Miss Beth was her brother would have fought him to the death. When all was said and done, he never went back to that job. I guess some situations call for extreme measures to resolve.

Evelyn enjoyed a good relationship with her stepfather Mr. Melvin until she got to be about fourteen and he started looking and acting very seductively towards her Evelyn. Miss Beth had the worrisome task of having to protect her daughter from sexual advancements made by her husband. To further complicate this horrendous game of cat and mouse Miss Beth's had to perform this drama in front of her elderly aunt who lived in the home too. Miss Beth found the duty of protecting her daughter from her husband physically draining, spiritually depressing and embarrassing. By the time Evelyn was sixteen Miss Beth was so frustrated with her husband's doggish behavior in pursuing her daughter that the thought of poisoning her husband was constantly on her mind. Miss Beth didn't actually want to kill him, she just wanted to let him know who she was, and the extent she was willing to go to make his behavior stop. Miss Beth's suspicions of her husband were not unfounded. Miss Evelyn told me she had many hurtful secret encounters with her stepfather because she had to get him straight quite a few times due to his inappropriate advances towards her. Evelyn said her stepfather used every opportunity when no one was around to expose himself and make nasty sexual remarks to her. Evelyn's stepfather, Mr. Melvin never let her uncle catch him because he feared her uncle would have killed him slowly. Unfortunately, Evelyn's uncle didn't live in the house, so her stepfather had plenty of opportunities to secretly make Evelyn's life dreadful. Evelyn, not wanting to embarrass her mother or cause her family to disintegrate over this horrible issue, handled it as best she could. Her stepfather was the sole provider so she decided she would endure this problem herself. Even though all the women in the family knew Miss Evelyn's stepfather secretly tortured her, nobody said anything as long as he never got a chance to physically touch her. They all endured this appalling situation for Miss Beth's sake. Women have tolerated this type of demeaning situation for what seems like since the beginning of time. It was a bittersweet experience for Miss Evelyn to have gotten married at the age of sixteen. But for the sake of everyone concerned, Miss Beth consented because this marriage would allow the entire household to finally exhale.

Once married, Evelyn's troubles started immediately. Her husband Richard had a restless spirit, and he was always dragging Miss Evelyn from one state to another. This restless spirit was also accompanied by a bit of a whorish behavior, but he never left home. But the worst trouble would prove to be Richard's illness that from the very beginning would cast a dreadful shadow on their entire lives.

Miss Evelyn was an only child by her mother and the illegitimate daughter of a rich absentee father who eased his mind by catering to all of Evelyn's physical needs. Miss Evelyn always knew she wanted to leave the small town she grew up in. So, in 1952, when her husband Richard suggested they give New York a chance she welcomed the opportunity. When Miss Evelyn arrived in New

York she had a baby in her arms and one in her belly, but she trusted her husband and she was not afraid of hard work. The car they rode to New York in, was a tad better than Jed Clampett's truck of the Beverly Hillbillies. When they pulled up in front of Evelyn's half-sister Diane's house, Diane was utterly amazed the car had come seven hundred and fifty-eight miles. Miss Evelyn was anxious to see her father, so without further ado or letting that hunk of junk they came in cool off, Richard, Evelyn, and Diane started for their father's house. After having traveled so many miles, in such an old vehicle it soon prove not to have been a wise idea to push such an old car to take another hour's drive. On the major highway to Rockland County New York during rush hour, the car started smoking and held up traffic for miles. The policeman who pulled them over said to Richard "Boy, why in the hell did you bring this piece of junk on a major thoroughfare?" Richard, being a country boy, his first time in New York City, and just being honorably discharged from the Navy, he was terrified of that city police officer. Richard was so ever humble, and Evelyn said he actually bowed when he addressed the officer. The policeman was so pleased he had finally met a Negro who knew his place and honored his White authority. Richard's bootlicking, and subservient posture was quite agreeable to the officer, so he helped them get to a gas station. Richard was feeling on top of the world. He had just narrowly escaped a good beat down that would have probably killed him and a book full of traffic violations. Besides, Richard couldn't imagine why they had referred to this great running car as a piece of junk. He had just bought that car all the way from the deep south. Once Richard got to the gas station, he was feeling so good he got out of the car grandstanding. He told a White gas attendant to "fill her up." The gas attendant was shocked this Negro thought himself so important to be giving him orders in such an authoritative voice. He told Richard "You are darn lucky boy I let you get gas! And you better hurry and take this piece junk out of my station." Richard told Evelyn to pay that cracker no mind. This car had been mighty good to them. Diane couldn't stop laughing and told Evelyn, finally, someone had corrected her husband and let him know he was not the president of the United States. Besides, Diane wanted Richard to know the car he was driving was by no means a Cadillac and it looked like something that had recently been torn away from a horse's hitch. Richard was seriously angry with Diane and threatened to leave her at the gas station. The gas attendant overheard Richard say he would leave Diane and told Richard "I will call the law on you boy if you don't leave and take all these niggers you brought here with you."

They finally reached Evelyn and Diane's father's Resort. Norman was also quite shocked Richard's old car had traveled such a far distance with only one incident. Norman made no real secret that he felt his daughter had followed her heart rather than her head by marrying Richard. Norman had made it big just like he always said he would. He had a head for numbers and became a bookie with the illegal numbers trade in Harlem. Norman had a stroke of luck on his side when he hit the numbers for a huge win and he immediately invested in a forty-acre resort located in the prime property of upstate New York. Just as many successful men before him, Norman's accomplishments did not come without tragedy and sorrow. Having escaped a painful and embarrassing scandal, Norman had strict rules concerning any deep emotional entanglements. Past events had shown him it was wise to only be faithful to those things that would be an advancement to his business. Norman stayed clear of any woman occupying a key job in his establishment. Norman knew a man would have no romantic design on him that would eventually become worrisome later when he no longer wanted that particular person to occupy that position in his company. A woman's suicide due to a breakup taught him women can become too attached and the burden of guilt and gossip could be a real career killer.

Norman knew having a great chef was crucial to the success of his business. Richard, his son-law had been trained in the Navy to be a chef and to everyone's surprise, he was quite gifted as a cook and in the art of baking. But alas, Norman prided himself on seeing a storm way out in the ocean and always did what was in his best interest no matter who got hurt. Richard's inability to maintain a firm diet kept him weak and sickly. So, Norman decided Richard would be used for a short time until a more suitable person could be hired.

Norman started the resort with two very flimsy buildings that were little better than shacks. He never did drugs and under no circumstances did he allow his little head to have the rule over the head on his shoulders. An exclusive sex transit hotel can quickly accumulate large amounts of that filthy Lucre, so in record speed, Norman turned that rat hole into a family vacation resort that became very well known in NYC and the upper state. After thirty years of running the resort, Norman became a wealthy entrepreneur. Of course, all that wealth brought many leeches, all looking to see what they could beg, borrow, or steal. When it came to money Norman was no fool. He was generous with his daughters to a point. Whenever they needed money for a large practical purchase Miss Evelyn and Diane could count on their father. Throughout Norman's life, because of his wealth, he had many women vying for his attention. Even though later in life he started to take on a Quasimodo look. None of these relationships ever amounted to anything more than a roll in the hay. Norman, however, did choose Patty. A woman who was willing to accept all of Norman's significant faults such as his insatiable drive to be a successful entrepreneur to enjoy the company and respect of other rich men, his inability to love and be loved, and his constant whoring with other women. Patty came from a very poor and hard background, so she learned early in life what most women require a lifetime to accept. She understood that only men could afford the luxury of romance. In the year 1995, Meryl Streep revealed in "The Bridges of Madison County " that millions of women have secretly endured the life of a non-passionate marriage so their offspring could enjoy a more successful life. Patty's life wasn't as meaningful as a penguin's existence. The story goes that a female penguin will always find her soulmate. But if his physical traits are not up to standard for her offspring, she will find a suitable surrogate to bring about the next generation. Instinctively, the female penguin will not live without real love, so she stays with her soulmate but will have no offspring from him. As women, we can learn quite a bit from the animal kingdom.

Patty and Norman's story were of two people working for selfish greedy goals that most times lead to destruction. Patty worked a grueling schedule of hard work, and she was also the butt of every joke Norman's family told. I don't know how, but Patty managed to give up all the things that make a woman pretty. Finally, after all she endured, Patty became Norman's right hand. She was now head chief over the resorts' kitchen but that came at a terrible price. Every day, Patty was dressed in a man's thread bear shirt, old khaki pants, and a ten-year-old wig she slapped on her head in no particular way. She also wore huge diabetic shoes so she could tolerate those 18 hours days on the hard cement floor in the poorly ventilated and extremely hot kitchen. Patty also secured her son James with the other strategic position at the resort. The job of bartender where he could control and steal vast sums of money. Norman had no idea how cunning Patty was. While he continued to be the front man of the business the real strings were being controlled by Patty. The resort would ultimately be owned by James' Jewish princess wife Donna.

Because Black men feel they will never die, they make no arrangements for their family's next generation. Later in life, Norman became senile and his stepson James along with his wife Donna quickly, and secretively, had Patty marry Norman. A few months later Norman suddenly died leaving all his wealth and the entire business to Patty. Who can stand against a marriage license? Surely not two blue-collar daughters with no finances for legal help. Now Patty, James, and the Jewish princess would see what happens when the fickle finger of fate starts to work really close with Murphy's law. About a month after Norman's death Patty passed away. Now the resort belongs to James and his lovely bride. A month after Patty passed away her dear son James had a heart attack and was left paralyzed. I guess all that free liquor and his whorish lifestyle caught up to him with horrible consequences. Long before the drool ever touches James' chest, his long-suffering Jewish princess wife has him committed to a nursing home. There James dies about a month later. The Jewish princess and her two mulatto daughters inherit everything Norman worked so very hard to attain. The Jewish princess with the help of her Hebrew uncle's lawyers had everything legally done and in order. She walked away free, clean, and a very rich woman.

When Miss Evelyn and Richard first arrived in New York Norman's resort was unable financially to employ them full-time. So, they decided to try Brooklyn where Richard's sister Gloria lived. Richard became ill and was unable to work when they first moved to Brooklyn. Gloria enjoyed having her younger brother and entire family depend totally upon her for their every need. Gloria had a very high and mighty personality and it thrilled her to no end to be in charge of these country bumpkins and show them a New York sophisticated life. Well, that might have been alright if that was all of the true story. Yes, Gloria had an ok paying job but that's where Gloria's wonderful storybook life ends. Gloria was married to Mack and he was a quiet and very particular man. In later years, I would realize Mack was homosexual. I am quite sure over the years his disdain for having to pretend came to an abrupt halt and left the marriage. Homosexuality in that era was not just in the closet it was kept in a deep dark dungeon that only the two parties involved ever visited. Why Gloria remained married to Mack was way beyond my understanding. Gloria and Mack lived in a sub-ground level kitchenette and shared a bathroom with another unfortunate family. I do believe this other family was in the worst condition because at least Gloria and Mac could look up out of a window and see the ankles of those who passed by. As for the other family, sadly they couldn't even see that. We can all agree it was not for the pleasures of high living that Gloria suffered this sexless marriage. Now Gloria did have her good points, both of my parents suffered the flu at one time, and she brought all of our Christmas and holiday dinner. Gloria taught my sister and me the responsibility of being a caring aunt.

Miss Evelyn had no ties or references to secure an apartment in Brooklyn, so she had to trust Gloria to find her family a place to live. Why Miss Evelyn committed this trusting act to Gloria after seeing her and Mack's apartment is beyond me. The only redeeming fact about this kitchenette apartment Gloria found for us besides being a solid roof over our heads, was that it was way above ground level. As a matter of fact, it was three flights above the ground. Now, for the rest of this very sad story. The only view this apartment offered was the backyards of very affluent Black people who had large pools and big stone barbecue pits. And of course, they entertained constantly. With nothing else to do my sister and I were their captive audience. We were too young to have any shame. So, with pure envy, we watched these rich people's outdoor activities whenever they entertained and drooled at the tasty bites they devoured. This harsh type of exposure to the rich is a two-sided coin. It will either inspire you to move up in life or to have a dreadful desire to eat the very hair off any rich person's head. Of course, hatred always causes imminent destruction. We give God the praise that both my sister and I didn't allow the fickle finger of fate to pull the strings and cause us to spiral down the drain. So, the best advice is to seek Jesus and be assured all will be well.

Once I got older, I realized just how tight money was for my family at that time in our lives. There was one incident in particular that comes to mind. My father had recently experienced a gout attack and he was unable to walk to the store and of course, my mother was at work. Being the older sister of a six-year-old I could go to the store alone, so my father waited for me to come home from school to spend a penny my sister had found in the house that day. But first, we must examine my sister's personality. My mother had to refrain from buying my sister balloons because of the total breakdown she had once her balloon would burst. My mother usually bought us both huge balloons that cost about twenty-five cents each. This purchase set her back by fifty cents which was a lot to spend at one time on a toy and my mother was a very thrifty person. She could hold a dollar until the eagle screamed. And I've had the misfortune of hearing him scream many times because even as a young child, I had some extremely lavish grownup requests. My mother was left with the dilemma either to buy another balloon that would eventually pop and endure this whole ordeal over again and be out of another quarter; or talk me into giving my sister my balloon and replacing it with something far less expensive, usually a small piece of candy. Now you will understand what a horrible thing I did to my poor sensitive sister that day. My father told me to take the penny and buy my sister something from the store that I knew she would like. At that time there were so many candies that could be purchased for a penny and I was overwhelmed with choices. You must remember I am only six years old with one lone penny. Well, my first thought of course was what did I like best, and my second thought was what could I buy that we could share. What I chose was not even candy. It was a very small clear piece of plastic with no type of flavor at all. It was shaped like a Coca-Cola bottle with a tiny amount of sweet colored water inside. Once I got my treasure outside the store I immediately bit the top off and put it to my lips but because it had such a strange little opening the liquid dribbled right down my chin. So now I am on my way home with this tasteless piece of plastic with not even a drop of sweet liquid left to present to my father and my water bag sister. What a dreadful situation I now found myself in. When I got home both my father and sister were devastated by the horrible deed I had committed. My sister had gone totally to pieces and my father only said in a small quiet voice that my sister had saved that penny all day long in anticipation of having a sweet treat. At least my sister cried therefore having a form of release. But my father knowing that he had put both his dear children in such a difficult situation made him ashamed that he was not able to provide the simple things in life for his precious daughters.

Miss Evelyn's family had to share a bathroom with three other families. A woman with a cleaning disorder had the very scary and annoying habit of meeting any occupant of the bathroom day or night to sanitize the facilities after each person's use. It was not the worst thing she could have done but it was just so humiliating to see her at every bathroom episode. Evelyn's family had the only TV in the building. So, every Saturday night, four humble men with no ability to save for a large ticket item would come to watch "Have Gun will Travel and Gunsmoke. These men had been living in the building for quite some time before we moved there, and they never bought a TV before we left. Richard loved being the big dog and they always came bearing jubilant brown bags of joy and I'm quite sure this added to the excitement of the evening. I know it made for bigger and better lies. For one and a half hours, these hopeless, oppressed Black men would strut their stuff, and stick their chests out like White men, with no fear of being laughed at or put in their place by a rich spiteful White man. It was a relief from the harsh reality of being a poor Black man in America. Saturday night TV was a special treat. I always pretended to be asleep so the men would be free to talk. I got to see the most popular shows on TV and I really loved hearing the lies they told. These were not just your run of the mill lies. Their lies were straight from their poor broken hearts. At the beginning of the night, they usually lied about the strength and stamina of their mighty peckers and how they juggled two and three women in one night. By the end of the night, each man had taken his turn at being Matt Dillon. The characters they played always took up the cause of the underdog and how they never allowed their White bosses to humiliate their Black workers. Their fantasies somehow made me proud, even though at my young age I knew they didn't have an "Am I born to die" attitude. If they wanted to keep those pieces of jobs they had better do as they were told no matter how degrading the situations were.

Miss Evelyn, though smart, was an unskilled worker needing money and of course, Richard was ill, so she took one of the most stressful jobs the labor market had to offer. Evelyn did piece work pressing shirts in a hot, poorly ventilated, and overcrowded dirty factory. The drive for steadfast production dehumanized the owners as well as the workers. Small infractions of the rules were severely dealt with by supervisors that took pleasure in embarrassing the unfortunate soul that had dared to break the rules. The job required you to be fast and efficient. The iron had to be hot to knock the wrinkles out fast but not too hot that it would burn the delicate material. If so, you would be out on your behind immediately.

Whenever the company found itself in a slow period people were fired. The only redeeming part of the job was it paid an excellent salary for that time. If you were able to hustle those shirts off that ironing board, there was money to be made. Miss Evelyn was very fast and efficient but there were always people at the job who found a way to beat the system. The rules were very simple, the floor lady was in charge of giving the bundles out to the pressers. But some pressers would hide easy bundles in various places or pretend they were almost finished. Therefore, they would get an extra easy bundle before others could get them. When that didn't work, they slipped the floor lady a few dollars to ensure they were given the easy bundles. It was a dog-eat-dog situation every day at the job because everybody had mouths to feed at home that were depending on them.

The stress of the job caused Miss Evelyn to have terrible nightmares that made her scream and cry in the most pitiful, childlike manner at least two to three times a week. These dreams were always about her mother's husband Mr. Melvin and his stomping footsteps coming down a long hall leading to her bedroom. Evelyn told us she never saw him in her dreams, but she knew it was him because one time he came into her room and she woke up while he was standing over her bed. I admire her courage to endure these dreadful dreams just to make a buck. Because if I had that dream, just one time, it would have scared the hell out of me to even think about going to sleep; and we all know we have to go to sleep eventually. It wouldn't have made a damn bit of difference to me who ate or who did not eat. I would have told that job goodbye baby after the very first bad dream and we would have all eaten whatever was in the house until I found another job.

Miss Evelyn was a smart woman with modern ideas and met every new decision at a slow, steady pace, doing only what she fully understood. But as most Black women, she never understood the spirit of slavery that hung over her head. An affluent woman feels a new baby inside her and she feels this could be the person to cure cancer or that solves the riddle for peace on earth. A woman of spiritual poverty feels a baby inside her and she whispers, "You sweet little thing." She has no hope for her baby's greatness, only that her child avoids trouble. These two attitudes mold and shape children in entirely two different ways. One has an entitlement for greatness and the other just tries to keep his head above water. We always got what we needed, and most of the time what we got what we wanted because Evelyn could make a dollar spend twice! Her husband Richard, at the young age of twenty-two, was afflicted with Gout. A chronic and acute disease that would severely punish him until his very death. There were no specific medicines for Gout at this time. Only treatments that eased the horrific attacks after weeks of suffering. Most people's Gout was centralized in one specific joint but unfortunately, Richard's affliction inflamed his entire body. Richard's illness kept him in constant poor health and therefore he was unable to provide financially for his family. This disease required a strict diet that he would never overcome. Richard's disease was also way ahead of medical science. At that time, doctors had a poor understanding of inflammatory and autoimmune diseases and there was no therapy. What we have to admit is that doctors are merely men with education and if there is anything you can do to help yourself then you had better damn well do it. Richard had a spirit of pride that he wore as if it were a medal of honor. This pride caused his family needless stress and strain because he refused to accept any financial help from the Veterans Administration. It was truly heartbreaking to see this disease twist and mangle his fingers until one day he no longer had hands, but only two deformed paws that by anyone's standards were useless. But day after day Richard would struggle with a crippled body and the shame of all his deformities, to try and hold a job to provide for his family. Eventually, he would succumb to the excruciating pain and be admitted into the hospital. Richard's employment usually lasted about six weeks. Never allowing him to establish any security at these jobs. With each admission to the hospital, a social worker would always set him up to receive financial benefits. The hospital always acknowledged the severity of Richard's disease and the deformities his body had undergone due to the disease. Once home, he immediately informed the Veterans Administration he was now out of the hospital and would soon be returning to work. After one such phone call, I saw Miss Evelyn cry one of the most defeated, heart-wrenching cries; pleading for Richard to accept help from the Veterans Administration. This damn pride of Richard's caused the family to barely keep their heads above water and was the same reason they had no car. Miss Evelyn had to take public transportation to do piece work ten hours a day in a hot, dusty sweatbox. Time accompanied by many bitter disappointments will eventually make you hear what life is saying. What your heart refuses to hear, God will use only a few words. And in an instant, He will reveal the whole truth. The illusion you carefully nurtured for twenty-five years to justify why your husband was so sick falls away. Miss Evelyn realized the pillars that supported her husband's pride might as well have been made from the salt of her tears. It became painfully clear that Negro loved to eat, and her husband couldn't resist the rich foods that were the cornerstone of this nightmare. To eat a pork chop, he was willing to endure extremely painful attacks that permanently left his joints twisted and snarled untilled his entire body was grotesquely disfigured. Richard's feet and hands were five-times their normal size because they were filled with pus that leaked out of his every joint. He reminded you of a tall stick figure that had huge, oversized boots for feet and massive oven mitts for hands. Can you imagine, he worked as a professional cook in this condition. A professional cook who they hid in the kitchen and wasn't paid his worth due to his handicap. In this same condition, he put on his only suit and accompanied me to school to defend a wrong I felt had been done to me. He was a wonderful father. Shortly after, Miss Evelyn realized her husband's true predicament was two diseases, a food addiction, and an acute case of gout. Richard, the love of her life passed away at the age of forty-five. Evelyn then walked away from her factory job and found a job with the state. That was quite a wonderful break for me because my mother now worked the third shift from eleven pm to seven am. It was on and poppin for me to live the life of freedom I so desired.

Miss Rudy

(Only Doing What They Understood)

In my first encounter with Miss Rudy, I knew immediately when fashion designers had nightmares, Miss Rudy played all the characters. An unattractive face has never discouraged a fashion designer but a room full of models with breasts the size of double H cups would cause concern for the bravest fashion designer. Miss Rudy saved six months' salary to buy her bras from stores that specialized in fine garments for large and ill-shaped women. The bras Miss Rudy wore always had her breast looking like two large fine trophies underneath a double-knit sweater. She felt her large breasts were a powerful weapon over any man's genitals and could make his mind flip another way. Miss Rudy had a very flat pinched behind and no stomach with a great pair of legs that were long and pecan tan. Miss Rudy did not own a dress that went below her knees. She was a woman who believed in working to the best of her ability with what God gave her. But from here, it all went downhill. Her face had many situations going on all at the same time. Such as not one symmetrical feature. She had a very broad face that made her keen features seem too far apart and a blotchy skin tone. In addition to these disorders, she had crepey dark circles around her eyes and within these circles were tiny black meat moles. She resembled an ugly raccoon with large pearly white teeth. Miss Rudy's head appeared even larger because her hair was short and sparse. Sometimes having the talent to use a professional curling iron can be a curse for a Black woman. Miss Rudy hot curled her hair every day and I know without a shadow of a doubt that is what burned her hair up. Miss Rudy was in a catch-22. Even though that fiery hot curling iron was destroying her hair, she needed her hair to be curled immaculately each day because without her hair being done to perfection she turned into the last hag.

Having the position of a school cafeteria supervisor and sporting those huge breasts, made Miss Rudy naturally bossy. Therefore, making her an overbearing bitch that very few people would care to boast as their friend. Having this job as cafeteria supervisor Miss Rudy was able to spend her money on the finer things in life, her weekend entertainment. The trivial task of picking up groceries from the supermarket would be left to those who could do no better. Her family's nutritional resources came from her place of employment therefore they ate the very best on the taxpayer's tab. Miss Rudy enjoyed quite a few perks. She frequently brought home entire turkeys and large tender roast portions of beef and huge bounties of can goods from her job. I never saw Miss Rudy or her children in the supermarket and whatever items that were not readily available from the school she borrowed without the least bit of reservation. Miss Rudy's food pantry could rival any top-shelf restaurant in New York. This habit of Miss Rudy borrowing everything she was not given or that she didn't steal from her job annoyed my mother to no end. My mother worked eight long hot hours pressing clothes at piece work speed and no one even gave her a handout. My mother decided that Miss Rudy's gravy train was no longer stopping at her station and we were forbidden to loan any of our hard-earned supplies.

Any sophisticated woman living in the projects did her very best to rake and scrape money to transform her project living room into a Louis the 16th sitting room. You have got to know these women were working with only a limited number of rooms. There was only one living room and you had better be careful how you sat your behind down on that sofa. Tipping over one of those fragile chandelier lamps could mean your behind. These French Provincial living room sets were not for the lazy. They required a woman's full attention. The sofas had fancy material and pleats with many buttons that were very tempting to small children. Children loved picking at the pleats and pulling off the buttons. It was a child's paradise. They were always trying to stuff tiny dirty toys into the pleats of the fabric. An innocent person could get into big trouble because these French Provincial living room sets were rigged with pain in the butt bobby traps. For example, you had to be careful when you passed by a sofa with decorative fringes because if one got stuck on a piece of your clothing or shoes you could accidentally cause those fringes to unravel, and now you are in the situation room. Every weekend my friends and I had to polish that decorative wood. There were many curves and you best not let that greasy liquid touch that fine white fabric, or you would have hell on your hands. Due to their competition for the best living room, Miss Rudy and my mother bought the same impractical colored sofa. A white pearl fabric that would become dirty just from the atmosphere of the house. "My Lord give me strength." The biggest offense that could be committed in the presence of these fine French Provincial sets was of course eating. But because I was so grown and thought I knew everything; I believed this directive didn't include me. But one dark day in my haste to answer the phone which of course is the life's blood for every teenager I spilled hot chocolate on the sofa. My mother was furious. She broke down and wept bitter tears. In my mother's world, I do believe the earth shifted on its axes and suddenly turned the other way, but I do know all the state flags should have been flown at half mast for me that day. Every woman that knew anything about cleaning came to the house to suggest how this awful world-changing disaster could be rectified. I was shunned by family and neighbors and it seemed I could hear them whisper, "That's the one who spilled the chocolate." This indeed was a serious matter. I was barred from the living room. I was only allowed to pass through to go to the front door or else I would be flogged. A week after this incident a Jewish man from the factory outlet where this fine furniture had been purchased; came and measured the living room set for plastic covers. Those plastic covers were most uncomfortable; cold in the winter, sweaty in the summer and, when that plastic became frayed, sharp edges developed with the ability to draw blood. Miss Rudy decided to live dangerously, and she never had her living room set covered with plastic. Miss Rudy's whole illusion of grandeur would have been destroyed if someone thought she could not afford the set in the first place, and you know that would never do. Miss Rudy had my vote. I say, "Go big or go home." My mother and Miss Rudy had a Travis rod that allowed them to use a drawstring to open and close their drapes just like rich white women did on Long island. I guess one of their friends that worked as a domestic worker told them about this awesome fashion feature in home decorating. Miss Rudy found a Hasidic Jewish factory outlet that had easy payment plans and had everything you needed to transform your living room and bedrooms into a marble museum. Can you imagine? These women raised four and five kids in these small apartments and this fragile furniture survived because in those days you had to listen to your parents or be killed?

As a child, I would have imagined Miss Rudy suffered greatly for she would have been a most unattractive child. To make matters worse, her sister Donna was blessed in all areas of beauty. She had a Barbie doll shape, was five feet nine inches tall, caramel skin, and had a striking resemblance to the model Iman. How good does it get? I have an inquisitive mind which my mother labeled nosey. I am always studying adults and one particular day I realized Miss Rudy had one too many drinks. This was a prime opportunity for me to question Miss Rudy fully about the big difference in her and Donna's appearance. Well, that alcohol really loosened up Miss Rudy's tongue and she unloaded her true family history. It was revealed, Donna was only a distant cousin. Donna was the last child of twelve children to be born to a woman that was at her breaking point. Donna's mother couldn't afford to care for her financially or mentally. Donna's mother brought her to Miss Rudy's mother's house late one night and begged to leave the baby there for only one night and said another cousin would pick baby Donna up the next day. Donna's mother then left and ran off with a guy who worked in the circus cleaning animal stalls. The next time they laid eyes on Donna's mother was about fifteen years later. Miss Rudy told me she hated Donna as a baby. Anytime Donna whimpered, Ms. Rudy's mother was there to attend to her every damn need and, if she wasn't available Miss Rudy had to take care of her. Miss Rudy's sister and brothers were all very brown skin children. Miss Rudy said her mother worshiped the very ground that good for nothing whore walked on just because she was "high yellow." Miss Rudy was in bitter tears when she told me how hard it was to study and work as a domestic worker when going to high school. Donna never bothered herself with work and didn't finish school. Donna filled Miss Rudy's mother's house with babies and could care less about what anyone thought. Because of this, Miss Rudy could never understand how her mother could love someone else's child so much more than her flesh and blood. Miss Rudy's mother's love affair with Donna never waned even though Donna turned out to be nothing. Donna had three babies out of wedlock and only halfway took care of Miss Rudy's mother in her old age. All of this was a very well-kept secret that wasn't even shared with Miss Rudy's children. I could barely contain myself until I got to my mother's ears.

As one who has also suffered the trauma of being an ugly child, I know Miss Rudy would have endured many painful remarks from cruel adults and outspoken children. Miss Rudy decided God had not given her beauty but brains and a triple portion of tits. So, through the years Miss Rudy learned to hide her insecurities behind a witty, sharp, sarcastic tongue. She deviously ridiculed anyone she thought could inflict her with the shame she had endured as a child. When you went out with Miss Rudy socially, she could be a friend and enemy all at the same time.

My mother told me she and Miss Rudy were at a bar called the Motor Club. Let me explain the Motor club so you can fully understand the fraudulent immorality that occurred there, in other words bull. The Motor Club was a place where Black transportation workers hung out to party. The men and women that frequented the club were in their forties and fifties but the men there were not worth the spit in your mouth. All the men were married, so we can agree this no place for children. The men that went to the Motor Club had salaries that afforded them just above a few dollars to spend on an outside woman, three drinks, and a chicken basket. Fifty years ago, these Motor Club men would be considered a cut above most other Black married men that only had their genitals to recommend them; and we all know they could be found by the dozen. Sad but true. Only the foolish women who were willing to believe they were favored to play the odds and win the exception to the rule, would have allowed their feelings to become seriously involved with any of these Motor Club men. These men loved their wives and to leave their homes never occurred to them no matter what those Negros said while indulging in the up and downstroke. If you were desperate enough and allowed your heart to seriously get involved with one of these Motor Club men, you could be assured of a bitter ending. These men had paychecks that barely covered their immediate family's needs, so it was definitely cheaper for them to keep their wives. Trying to shack up with one of these motor club men a woman could find themselves helping some Negro to pay child support. These were only toy boys and nothing else.

Two young women at the Motor Club were enjoying the attention of all the men in the place. Miss Rudy told my mother "Watch this Evelyn." Miss Rudy took off her coat and presented those double H cups under a tightly knitted sweater and that's all she wrote. Miss Rudy and my mother had the attention of every man in the place. You better believe those titties had power over most men and all those who had a few drinks. Even if huge breasts were not a man's M.O. that freaky curiosity in him would just want to see something that big. If things were going Miss Rudy's way, she would be my mother's best buddy. But if the crowd started being more attentive to anyone else, even to my mother, Miss Rudy's wrath would start up and you might be in for a very embarrassing night. In Miss Rudy's thirst to be a big shot whenever her money dried up, she would start to manipulate others into spending their money on those she wanted to impress. Usually, she was successful because she was such a good bull jive artist. But when she tried to get my mother Miss Evelyn to front a bar bill boy did, she get a surprise. My mother told Miss Rudy "You better have the money for those drinks you set these people up with. I don't play that junk. I'm not looking to impress no cheap behind man by buying a bunch of drinks for these no good for nothing Niggers." That was the last time Miss Rudy tried that trick with my mother.

If Miss Rudy was to be the smartest person in the room, there were sacrifices to be made and she gladly expected the challenge. Her cold calculating plan for being a star in society meant she could only watch the news and educational TV. This fixation gave her the ability to work in the largest room of people with ease. Miss Rudy knew she had many gifts to offer a man, an inviting smile, a challenging conversation about current events, and hours of understanding talk about his job. Miss Rudy could make the wimpiest man feel robust when she had finished with him. Miss Rudy's had the great ability to zoom in on a woman's most fragile feature and turn it into a great compliment that could boost a woman's ego out of this world. Once, she found a woman at a party that could cool your soup in seconds because of her incredibly large lips. Miss Rudy complimented the woman by telling her every man in the room was imagining her deeply kissing him and sending him to the moon. This would have been a woman probably too shy to flaunt the great sex appeal she possessed. Everyone in the room wanted to speak with Miss Rudy even though she looked like a raccoon with pearly white teeth. A strong powerful personality can overcome all sorts of obstacles. I always told my mother Miss Rudy should have been a politician because she had the gift of BS.

That deadly sarcastic tongue made her a formidable foe for those she perceived to be weak. Her specialty was embarrassing women that were attractive, and when she felt they were receiving too much attention from the crowd. Of course, she hid this under a thin veil of "I am just joking." This spiteful strategy worked like a charm because women were usually too afraid or embarrassed to challenge Miss Rudy. You had to be quick and have a razor-sharp tongue to bring it to Miss Rudy. If your comebacks were not strong enough to shut Miss Rudy down, she instantly would eat you alive. One night after going out with Miss Rudy my mother woke me up and told me Miss Rudy was slapped senselessly by a woman that had no come back except her righteousness right hand. Miss Rudy said something very funny about the woman's teeth, but her trusty thin veil of "I am just joking" didn't fly that time. At last, everyone at the club saw that sharp tongue of Miss Rudy's gets what it justly deserved. To make matters worse, the woman left immediately after the slap, so no one at the club got to be a witness to the police procedures that might have occurred. Because the woman left so quickly, she escaped without being arrested. Pressing charges against the woman might have erased some of the embarrassment of having all those people at the club see her get slapped and being helped up off the floor. But at last, Miss Rudy didn't have the pleasure of seeing the women being handcuffed or arrested. No one knew the woman's name or address, so for all intents and purposes, the woman who slapped and embarrassed the hell out Miss Rudy got away scot-free. This must-have left a lasting impression on Miss Rudy because my mother said Miss Rudy seemed a little more cautious from then on when she was addressed by strangers.

Miss Rudy was such a know-all and she never failed to capture an opportunity to show off her knowledge, whether right or wrong. We all were experiencing a phone outage in our area. When they started to fix the outages, you can believe they didn't start in the ghetto. I guess somebody has to be last. Miss Rudy was keeping company with two married men that had few chances to get out, so telephone communication was crucial to her good times. Our phone service had gone out before Miss Rudy's and it took about three days before we got our service back. Miss Rudy told Miss Evelyn, "I can't possibly be without my phone for the weekend! Somebody has to fix my phone immediately! It's ridiculous to wait three days. She said, "Evelyn, you have to be stern with them and let them know who they are talking to!" She stated, "I am going to get on the phone with them and when I finish, they're going to fix my phone today!" Of course, Miss Rudy was using our phone because she had no service. I heard Miss Rudy tell them the lie that she had a sick mother at her house and she really needed her phone to be in service. They told her they would make every effort to be there at noon. Well, you know what happened, noon came and went with no phone service or repairmen. Miss Rudy now tells Ma Bell she needs to speak to a supervisor, and she was not playing around. She waited on hold for an hour and a half. My mother and I found Miss Rudy very amusing. When she got off the phone with Ma Bell, Miss Rudy was quite confident her phone would be working by three pm as promised. Once again, Miss Rudy lectured all of us that she knew how to handle big companies because she was a supervisor at her job and knew how to delegate and speak with authority. It was now 4:30 pm and no phone repair personnel had arrived or called our phone to leave Miss Rudy a message. Miss Rudy was at her wit's end. The reality that she would probably be without a phone had started to set in. Miss Rudy started to concede defeat but decided to call Ma Bell one more time. It's now 4:45 pm, and Miss Rudy is huffing and puffing about the promises they had made. My mother and I were standing around listening to her hopeless pleas when we heard someone in the background say, "Just tell her we're on the way." Miss Rudy turned around as if she had just received a lifeline and told us "See I know how to tell them and I don't take any foolishness." The door closed behind Miss Rudy as she left the apartment. My mother turned with a look of sincerity and said to me sarcastically "We are on our way!" We both laughed until we cried. Miss Rudy's phone was restored late Tuesday of that coming week.

Miss Rudy was starved for that Sunday kind of love, but it was always out of her grasp. Her blessing in romance would be blocked for a lifetime due to her having a big shot know it all spirit, combined with a dumb Dora perception of reading men. Being such a know it all, she refused to abandon her "get a man to marry me" techniques. Her big shot attitude made her such a sucker for men and the people she wanted to impress. She thought she could lure a man away from his wife with flashes of riches she couldn't afford. Miss Rudy could have shown Fats Dominion a thing or two about a "Blue Monday." Her foolish spending on the weekend caused her many a blue Monday morning. On Monday morning's Miss Rudy woke up ashamed, broke, and defeated. All the people she thought were beneath her also shared a common predicament; they too were all broke as hell. Her Pride kept her from borrowing money because she would rather eat out the garbage can than let anyone know she did not have an "Am I born to die" on a Monday morning. Being broke after the weekend and having no train fare during the spring and summer just meant a long walk to work; but the winter was a different story. Sometimes she would swallow her pride and borrow money from her mother. That was a most dreadful little venture because her mother had a six sense about her daughter and knew exactly why Miss Rudy was in this predicament. Her mother never failed to give Miss Rudy a long humiliating lecture about her biggity ways. When she couldn't face her mother, she would have to walk, sometimes making her quite late to work. Thank God it wasn't too far but one particular morning Miss Rudy miscalculated the coldest of the weather. Underneath the sidewalk dirt and grime was treacherous black ice that snatched her behind down on to the pavement. Her inappropriate shoes for the weather caused her to slip and twist her ankle when she landed on the ground. This was the only catastrophe I knew about, but New York winters can be brutal. I would venture to say her overspending caused her to suffer many cold and blue Monday mornings. Sunday afternoons were also rough. Miss Rudy spent hours waiting for the phone to ring hoping and praying one of her worthless men would call her back, but then again, she had only been a good time booty call. These men were busy with their families enjoying that Sunday kind of love. My mother always told me it was hard and next to impossible to take a man away from his wife no matter what sexual acts he might have enjoyed during his booty call. Miss Rudy continued to throw her money at married men and never separated them from their beloved wives. "My God, please give me the strength to endure listening to such a sad story."

On Thursday night Miss Rudy would usually talk to the girls in the building. She would serve us homemade apple pie and whatever we wanted to drink. Her lessons were usually hardcore and quick and to the point. The girls in the building were aging into older teenagers and had questions about relationships with men. With Miss Rudy's help, us girls immediately knew the mode of operation various men used when visiting the women in the projects. Such as the jive talkers, the married men with lazy wives who always wanted to know if you had you anything to eat, the cheap and stingy men that never stopped at the food or liquor store before coming over, and the scaredy cats who were late riders not wanting to be seen but that booty call had a strong enticing power. These married men decided the women in the projects had needs and they would be the ones to fulfill them.

All these men proudly served in the booty call brigade fulfilling their duties in the brightest of day and the darkest of night. I often wondered did they take the post office oath because I have seen Negros come over a women's house on the snowiest of blizzards when they wouldn't have ventured forth to work in. Somebody had to service the ladies.

Miss Rudy had two very married boyfriends. Mr. Jackson whose wife worked during the day and Mr. Rivers' wife who worked late night into the morning. These men had to strictly adhere to their wife's good pleasure to keep these undercover rendezvous trouble-free. Private love making opportunities were really difficult to achieve making them far and few between. There were many obstacles to overcome. Miss Rudy had two young curious teenage girls and a man that could only visit during the day with limited funds for a hotel. The only place to entertain her gentlemen callers was behind a closed, cheap project bedroom door while trying to have silent sex. But that day, she had an unexpected visit by Mr. Jackson. The thought of having sex without being under a gag order was so exciting. Even though Miss Rudy knew her children Gail and Coco would be home in fifteen minutes the need to feel like a young woman again was overwhelming. At that moment, her vagina felt like it was going to burn her panties right off her body. The plan was my mother would tell Miss Rudy's children she had to run out and they were to stay at our house. Now this was highly unusual because Miss Rudy was always home from work by three o'clock sharp. With Coco and Gail, we now had six girls at our house playing records and inhaling everything in the refrigerator. After about several hours my mother was sick of us. Gail and Coco started complaining about the special snack they always ate when they got home and continued to annoy my mother about when their mother would come home. Then Gail piped up and said, "I think my mother is home." That's when our friend Regina said, "I know how to lift the peephole so we can see inside the apartment." We told my mom we were going outside, and she was so happy she could have gotten up and did the Boogaloo. My mother told me she hated teenagers with a passion. She was truly sick of all the noise and complaining. We quietly went next door to Miss Rudy's and Regina lifted the peephole. Miss Rudy and Mr. Jackson must have been taking a break because there they were stark naked in the kitchen where all of us had eaten many good meals. When Gail and Regina with their young tight curvaceous bodies saw the two old wrinkles butts and droopy titties they screamed! I guess it was a horrible look into the future. They had only seen Miss Rudy's breasts when lifted up by those fine expensive bras. Those big huge jugs were a horrible sight. They were flat as pancakes by her arms, and they looked like two long stretched out water balloons that covered her vagina. It truly was a hideous piece of business. Gail and Regina could barely believe what they saw. They scrambled away from the door laughing and giggling. My mother heard the commotion and came out our door wanting to know what was going on. All of us were silent and began running down the hallway towards the stairs. But Miss Rudy's had heard us looking through the peephole. Being a mom, she was quick. She composed herself and before we made it to the first floor she screamed down the hallway that Coco and Gail were to carry their behinds to their grandmother's house and stay there until she came to get them. Miss Rudy was furious with everybody including my mother for allowing her girls to come over to the house. When we got home my mother was demanding to know who had opened Miss Rudy's peephole. Needless to say, we had no Idea.

Miss Rudy was married and separated a long time before our families met. Her husband Mr. Rudy had an alcoholic disease that reduced him to sleeping in the gutters and the hallways of the projects. At one time, Mr. Rudy was an extremely handsome and responsible electrician. Miss Rudy told my mother her husband used to be a good-looking man before alcoholism and that he resembled one of her present boyfriends. I am quite sure good looks was Miss Rudy's main attraction to her husband.

When Miss Rudy's mother passed away, Mr. Rudy managed to clean himself up in order to attend the funeral and I saw why his daughters were so beautiful. It was definitely Mr. Rudy's genes that made those girls so attractive.

Mr. Rudy was known throughout the projects as the man that begged for coins in front of the liquor store. He did this in a clear view of Miss Rudy's window. Whenever Miss Rudy looked out her window, Mr. Rudy was sleeping on the benches or fighting with other winos about one drink or another. Mr. Rudy lived on the other side of the projects and knew many other winos over there. But he always invited his friends to come over to Miss Rudy's side of the project to drink and carry on. They sometimes drank with Mr. Rudy until all hours of the night. He knew no words he could possibly say to Miss Rudy would hurt her as much as having him being a public jackass for all of her friends to see. I have got to commend Coco and Gail. These two teenage girls showed a deep love for their father. These girls endured unquestionable embarrassment when struggling with their father's dead weight. They retrieved him out of the grass and off project benches. This task was not done in the dead of night but in broad daylight for all the greedy eyes in the project to see.

Miss Rudy said "Gail and Coco, you should call the police on your father. It's only out of the kindness of my heart and for the sake of you girls that I am allowing your father to stay and help take care of your grandmother. You girls know I provide him with free room and board." None of this was done out of the kindness of Miss Rudy's nonexistent heart. Miss Rudy's real agenda was using Mr. Rudy's disability and union pension checks to bankroll her ghetto fabulous weekends. Miss Rudy enjoyed her husband's money and he lived on nothing more than canteen money per month. All things were working in Miss Rudy's favor. She had her husband by the short hairs, and she consoled her daughter this BS. Miss Rudy said, "If I gave your poor father more money, he would drink himself to death within six months. You girls only have me to thank for keeping your father alive thus far. It's a true burden for me to oversee his financial affairs."

Miss Rudy outwardly loathed Mr. Rudy. She felt everything in her life that was wrong was her husband's fault and she hated him for it. When they first moved to the projects, Mr. Rudy gave Miss Rudy prestige as a married woman living a coveted life in a sea of single desperate women. Miss Rudy watched many aspiring young couples move into the projects using it as a stepping stone into a life on their way to homeownership. Unfortunately, Miss Rudy would see many come and go fulfilling their dreams. An alcoholic husband, along with too many extravagant weekends, and no savings, would only allow Miss Rudy to leave the projects in a body bag. Every time she saw her husband in a drunken stupor, it reminded her of why she was now searching for a Mr. Goodbar at the age of fifty-five. She might have had more luck capturing a unicorn in downtown Brooklyn. On one of our Thursday night talks with the girls, Miss Rudy said she had hitched her wagon to a losing horse. Miss Rudy also said, if a man tells you he does not drink, leave that alone and be thankful. Miss Rudy had forced her husband to have his first drink trying to impress some friends and you see how that turned out.

Once I had a date with an older man. I was about seventeen and he was twenty-eight. It was a real thrill because he was a recording celebrity. His band had just had their first big hit record on the R&B chart. He was playing at a club my friends hung out at. But first I have to tell this little story about what would always happen when the girls and I would go out. I didn't mind letting a man know there were plenty of other fish in the sea that were very interested in me. The more a man would "sweat me" the more I would swing my long fake ponytail at other men. A man once told me; guys would need big balls to even ask me to dance.

Our friend Nancy was about two hundred and sixty pounds. I know that because she told me under the strictest of confidence. Every time we all went to parties or clubs, Nancy always got the guys involved in conversation when she immediately entered the club. Now Nancy was attractive, and she knew how to apply her makeup really well. She wasn't the prettiest girl in our crowd, but her personality never failed a man. A few men would start swarming around her and I did not learn until this year, that men saw her as an easy mark for a one-shot sex night because of her size. They felt it wouldn't be much work or effort to win her confidence before they bed her down. I don't know if she ever caught on to their evil plan.

Now back to my situation. My mother was now working the second shift, so when my twenty-eight-year-old R&B artist picked me up she would be at work. The plan was going quite well. He had a lovely car, and I was his star. Since my mother would be at work when he came to pick me up there was one little condition; Miss Rudy had to meet him before I could go on the date and I thought all was not lost because Mrs. Rudy was more liberal than my mother. But I was going to find out Miss Rudy was way more liberal than I would imagine. As luck would have it, when my R&B star went to meet Miss Rudy she appeared to have just gotten in from somewhere else. Miss

Rudy's eyes lit up as I introduced her to my date, and she insisted that we come in and chat. I thought to myself well it's alright to go in and have a little chat. But then it hit me. I remembered what my mother said about Mrs. Rudy's talent of engaging men in conversation and making them feel they were the smartest man alive. As soon as we entered her apartment, she broke out the hard liquor lickety-split and I was only accustomed to a Virgin Tom Collins. I was never much of a drinker and that's why men found it hard to impress me at a bar. I never wanted anything except soda. I could see I was about to witness Mrs. Rudy's talents of truly engaging a man firsthand. My date was mesmerized by her attention and those big double H size breasts seemed to have taken on a life of their own right before my very eyes. My troubles were all around me. As chance would have it, CoCo and Gail were hanging out somewhere, and this left me alone to deal with this she-devil. Mrs. Rudy had the playing field and it looked as if I was never going to recapture the ball. If Miss Rudy or my date had anything to do with it, I could have just dropped off the face of the earth. I noticed they were no longer talking to me at all. I suddenly heard his thoughts, "Why should I waste my time trying to get her into bed. Who knew how many dates it would take? Whereas this big jug mama would jump me right there on the coffee table. She is begging for me!" I had to think fast, so I immediately stood up and acted as if I had stumbled and knocked over the soda and the ice. Miss Rudy ran to get towels to clean the mess off her precious rug and I told him I felt dizzy and would need some air right now. So off we went to the elevator. My Lord was with me and the elevator was waiting. Mrs. Rudy came running out of her apartment but a little too late. The elevator's sliding doors had made its connection and I hollered up to her as the elevator descended that we had to be on our way. That was a close one. I failed to mention Miss Rudy still managed to demonstrate her motherly instincts despite all of the lust she showed towards my date. She clearly mentioned twice how young I was compared to my date. His career was really starting to take off and no jailbait was going to derail him. He took me to dinner, bought me a necklace, and brought me straight home. Never to date me again.

Miss Jones

(Only Doing What They Understood)

Miss Jones was a country woman who lived her life unaware that she spiritually had the burden of a broken leg. She had been living in the Marcy for about a year when I first met her. Miss Jones was nothing to write home about. I would have to say the highlight of her life was having the courage to move to New York looking for a better life. Miss Jones was brought up in a very strict religious Baptist home where their mother took them to church nightly. I believed Miss Jones got married so young because that was the only way out of her mother's house. Miss Jones must have developed her rhythm and rhyme speech patterns by listening to different Baptist pastors during her childhood every night at church. Her mother never guessed that her daughter's claim to fame would be her ability to cuss and insult anyone she pleased poetically. When I met Miss Jones, she led an-uninspiring life with no Christian influences. Miss Jones' only God was a can of Colt 45 with a pack of cigarettes and of course Motown. She, unfortunately, married a very deceitful frog instead of a prince and conceived four extremely unattractive boys. She and her four boys all seemed to have narrowly escaped having that awful small head syndrome. Miss Jones was addicted to cigarettes and I assumed she smoked them throughout her pregnancies. Even though she and the entire nation had been warned by the Surgeon General about cigarette smoking affecting babies' birth weight and I think their head circumferences. But with her and others like her, warnings from health officials are ignored due to ignorance, traditions, and old wise tales. Miss Jones' physical appearance was ordinarily dull. She had a very small face with little fisheyes. Her face looked like Louis Armstrong without the extreme puffed-out cheeks, so you know we're not talking about a beauty queen. Miss Jones had jet black smooth skin which was her best asset but during this time in history, no one thought that was anything to be proud of or to even mention having black skin in a positive light. Miss Jones seemed to have a two-dimensional body that reminded me of a paper doll. She had snake hips and very skinny legs that were at the extreme edge of her body. She had very short cotton-like hair that would nap up with the least hint of humidity; thank God she had mastered the art of fixing her hair. She had thin lips with nice teeth but no clue about makeup to enhance her features. She wore a size 14 and stood 5ft. 8in" in her stocking feet therefore whatever she put on usually looked very nice.

Miss Jones's children's nutritional and clothing needs were met so she felt that her job was well done. Miss Jones and her husband kept to themselves and I very rarely saw her husband. I would not have known him on the street even though they live on the same floor as my family. Living on the sixth floor would prove to be a huge disadvantage for Miss Jones because her young children would require her escorting them whenever they went outside to play. This should not have presented such a hassle but laziness, ignorance, and Miss Jones having to give such serious attention to her illegal number playing she had little time for anything else. Miss Jones found it crucial to be able to speak intelligently about soap operas with the other ladies and her sisters back home. Watching and analyzing soap operas interpreting the number forms to be prepared when the number man comes to take your bets can leave little time for nurturing children. Then of course there was always that aggravating dinner meal that had to be attended to every day the Lord sent. Because her children very seldom went outside, they never really assimilated with the rest of the neighborhood children and they were always like fresh meat to vicious dogs every time they went out to play. Miss Jones was having to constantly yell out the window reprimanding the children to stop hitting and bothering her boys. This bullying situation would have cleared up in a New York minute had her four boys ganged up together and fought back. Most people don't have an appetite for a real fight; they only want to indulge if there is easy prey on the menu. Therefore, Miss Jones kept her children upstairs in the apartment other than school. These four boys were hell on her furniture and appliances. New bedroom sets were bought every six months. Once a year Miss Jones bought another cheap living set and stereo equipment. Miss Jones managed to keep the furniture that long only because she wore those boy's behinds out about tearing up her stuff, but boredom drove them to destroy anything they could get their hands on.

Only after a short while of knowing Miss Jones she came over Monday night after a three-day holiday wanting me to babysit her boys. Miss Jones informed my mother that her husband had taken all his clothes with him on a supposedly three-day trip to his mothers in Alabama. Of course, I listened to the whole conversation without my mother or Miss Jones' knowledge but by this time I had already learned a valuable lesson and I kept my mouth shut. Miss Jones decided to get out in front of this abandonment by going down to the welfare office early Tuesday morning. We all knew she would automatically get welfare seeing how she had been left with four boys, no education, and was clueless how to maneuver in a work environment. The babysitting job went without a hitch. The Welfare dept had given her a month's check, a shopping cart full of USDA food but the most important item in this bounty was an auburn wig she bought from the hair store. Make no mistake this was no ordinary wig, it was magic. In Miss Jones' mind, this wig did amazing things. It lifted the burden of that spiritual broken leg that had been with her forever so long. This wig had the power to correct all of her poor choices in life. But in her mind, the best gift of all was this wig that gave Miss Jones the life of being a high yellow woman with all of its privileges. life was on big time and hot as fish grease. Jame Brown told us exactly who she had become "A Sex Machine." This wig gave her confidence, and she was no longer forced to view the world with hooded eyelids. With her new identity, she could now look eye to eye with any woman or anyone for that matter. Because she now felt like a high yellow woman with power. This wig gave her social power to compete with other women and sexual power over men. Miss Jones had taken a new motto on in life from a record called "In the Summertime" by Mungo Jerry. Miss Jones lived by this record's lyrics that went like this "We're not bad people, we're not dirty, we're not mean, we love everybody but do as we please." Miss Jones went from being a quiet reserved housewife to one of the most sought after women in the projects. Every man in the projects wanted to tame this wild horse. No woman's husband was safe unless Miss Jones just didn't want him. Men had sex with her just for bragging rights. The only thing that kept her tied to that apartment was her real concern for her children's welfare. Miss Jones understood that her lifestyle demanded that she be totally independent of a man financially so, therefore, she had to stay in government-assisted housing.

As I said earlier, Miss Jones felt her children's nutritional and clothing needs were met so as far as she was concerned, she was doing a good job as a mother. Unfortunately, Miss Jones did not understand that a child's psychological well-being was just as important as their physical if not more. Miss Jones was a harsh disciplinarian and if she lived during these new times Miss Jones would have been under mandatory counseling or Child Welfare Services might have had her children removed. These boys had quite a few situations to man up to; that their mom was abusive, and she was the very worst type of whore in the project. Miss Jones had sex with men that were available and those that were totally taboo which were her neighbor's husbands. Miss Jones allowed men to live with her for maybe six months or just when they got thoroughly comfortable. I sincerely think it gave her a super thrill to see the shocked look on their faces when she told them without any notice that they would be leaving her apartment that very hour. They had two choices: they could go quietly, or she would call the police and have them escorted the hell out of her apartment. Once the police came, I am quite sure these men really wished they had taken the choice of just leaving when Miss Jones said to go. The send-off with the cops was always quite humiliating because they usually had to endure being publicly cussed out and her performances always divulged their sexual deficiencies. Because we lived on the same floor as Miss Jones, we always had a ringside seat to these events. Therefore, our experience was always a real treat because Miss Jones was a very entertaining rapper long before The Sugar Hill Gang. All the girls in the building marveled over the way Miss Jones could cuss you out with such precision and wit. Miss Jones was so very artful at weaving insults with curses that she could have been the envy of some of the most famous rappers of today. Miss Jones' opening line was "Hell no this is not going to work." Perhaps those that tried to debate with her really had nowhere to go at that moment or were just in amazement of being asked to leave a place where they had called home for the last six months. But of course, all of their begging, and logic about why they should not be made to leave at that moment, I knew was fruitless. Miss Jones spared a man no mercy. It was always her express duty to expose his shortcomings in the bedroom. She expressly explained how sickening it was to have endured his skinny black penis night after night. Her other pet peeve was his inability to hold an erection as long as she thought was sufficient. She always called the offenders of this awful crime "A quick draw negro." The lineup was always the same. First the man, then the two police officers and Miss Jones bring up the rear rapping and rhyming insults that told us what a disappointing son of bitch he had been. One of these episodes had to be the most embarrassing and hurtful situation any man could bear. It was a hot summer day in the projects, and everybody was sitting on the benches. Children were playing, teenagers were courting, and adults were getting their numbers right that they would later play. Miss Jones was furiously cursing and throwing her current boyfriend's clothing out of her window. I always thought that Miss Jones' personality was way too strong for this particular man to handle and I often wondered what made that relationship work, but it would be revealed that day to us all. He was picking up his clothes in silence and with much humility was pushing his belongings into a brown paper shopping bag. Miss Jones shouted to the very top of her voice, *"You used to make my whole-body quiver, when you went downtown – to the secret garden – but your ass can't even do that right anymore!"* passionate way a man can satisfy a woman, but you can't even do that now." And with those final words, Miss Jones slammed her window shut never to return that day. She was a bad Mama Jama. There were only a few things left on the ground after the window closed and he just continued to pick them up while the entire courtyard audience roared with laughter. Once all the clothes had been gathered this poor humiliated soul just walked around the corner.

The laughter had become infectious so whenever someone repeated what had been said by Miss Jones it became even funnier than the first time they heard it. The children somehow knew whatever Miss Jones had said was scary and forbidden. The teenagers who were still playing around with sex knew this was definitely uncharted territory. As for the grown men and women, well no one would dare in the light of day admit they had oral sex or had their vagina eaten. This was truly a shocking tale. What Miss Jones shouted out of the window that day was like a shot that was heard around the world but in this case, it went around the projects. By the end of the day, everyone had said the phrase out loud or whispered it to themselves. This phrase was told to all those who were not there to witness it for themselves. Weeks later, whenever someone in the projects did something stupid, or did something they should have known better or did something remarkable the phrase would be said, and of course it was still funny. Any incident that embarrasses someone else, people always like to keep on layaway to recall at the proper time. Now that Miss Jones had her 15 minutes of fame she settled back into her routine of whoring and partying.

Coming up in the projects my friends and I had the benefit of learning many survival tactics from the women in the building that nurtured us in the ways of life. Each woman had a particular skill set. Miss Jones only had sex for mutual enjoyment. A man was never going to take anything of value away from her and her children. And no way in the world would she allow a man to take money away from her and her children. Miss Jones' favorite statement when dealing with the overall care of her children was, "My children will always have toys for Christmas." Therefore, she considered herself an excellent mother no matter how whorish her behavior was in the community. Miss Jones thought it was disgraceful if a mother allowed her children to suffer lack because she was taking care of a man. Once, Miss Jones threatened to turn her good friend Annie into Child Welfare if she didn't put her boyfriend out of the house. Miss Jones had gone to Miss Annie's house during the day and her boyfriend was still in bed during a weekday.

After questioning the children, Miss Jones found out this man had never worked since he was living with Miss Annie. The children also told Miss Jones that they ate cereal every night and that Miss Annie and that Man ate regular food. Well, this infuriated Miss Jones and she told Miss Annie that her boyfriend would have to leave that evening. Miss Annie told Miss Jones to mind her own business and to leave her house. Miss Jones left immediately and returned with the police and they in turn reported Miss Annie to Social Services and she was pressured to put her boyfriend out. Miss Annie never spoke to Miss Jones again, but Miss Jones kept a better eye on Miss Annie and her children than Child Welfare could ever imagine. Miss Annie moved to another project in order to escape Miss Jones' watchful eye. But it was to no avail because Miss Jones found out where she lived and let Miss Annie know under no uncertain terms she would report her if the children were being neglected. Miss Jones told Miss Annie "My children will always have toys at Christmas as long as I live and yours better have them too."

I believe loneliness and pride can cause a woman to form a relationship with a man that she does not love. Most times, this man would be called the "safe man" because he had a weaker personality than hers and she felt that his cheating on her would not be a factor; and if she cheated, she would know how to keep it under control. So, you would think with all these factors working in her favor what could possibly go wrong. Well, let me tell you those safe relationships can cause you to just hate that weak man and you eventually eat him up and spit me out with unbelievable satisfaction. I have experienced a few relationships with a "safe man" and I could only tolerate them at best for about two weeks. I think your tolerance level is tied very closely with the amount of social and financial responsibilities you have at a particular time. Miss Jones was a very domineering woman, and most men were just not strong enough to manage to love her and remain a real man. I also feel most strong men would not have wanted a woman that was so bold with heavy drinking and cussing people out at the least provocation.

As the story goes, Miss Jones meets Johnny at the mailbox on Saturday morning which meant he was off from work. Johnny had beautiful skin and was a tall slender man that was relatively good-looking. But unfortunately, this is the only upside of the story. First of all, he was the product of a bipolar mother that self-medicated with quite a bit of alcohol and that kept her in all types of loud disputes with one neighbor or another. The man that lived with them only darted in and out of their apartment to go to work, so I never got a good look at him. He was so quick that I only got a glance and I know that was more than he wanted anyone to get. Johnny's younger brother was constantly in trouble in school and finally dropped out, which was a mutual separation between him and the school system. I heard that every girl in his class was now relieved to be rid of his continual harassment. He got into trouble and ended up in a boy's reform school. It must have been a low security facility because he just walked right off the premises and escaped back home. There he met his final demise by becoming one of the many victims of the heroin brigade that had been swept through the Marcy Projects that year. Johnny only left his house to go to work and to walk a very large female German Shepherd that the street committee said was his secret lover. I personally had never heard Johnny or knew anyone else in our building that heard him say a complete sentence. One late Saturday night coming from a party he was sitting on the bench with that huge animal. Now, don't hear me say I have never seen an owner kiss their dog, but the way Johnny caressed that dog I just got to believe there was more than ownership going on between Johnny and that Shepherd.

Miss Jones had to be out of her mind to get involved with Johnny. None of the girls in the building could hardly believe their affair. I am now convinced, all of the men after Miss Jones' husband abandoned her were "safe men" because she never wanted to feel that hurt again. Johnny was totally unstable and after becoming intimate with Miss Jones he felt he finally had the girl of his dreams. Someone just like his very own mother. Both Johnny's mother and Miss Jones had the same problems, heavy drinkers, very loud bold women, and they shared a love for telling people off in a lowdown dirty way. Like all of the safe men before Johnny, his end day had also come to an end with Miss Jones. I heard he broke down and wept. But it was to no avail because once a safe man has put the last straw on the camel's back there is no turning around. It requires love to hold a relationship together or a mother's sacrificial love for her children's sake to stay with a safe man.

After crying for some time, Johnny quietly left Miss Jones' apartment, went straight to the Brooklyn bridge and jumped to his death. Johnny's mother had a nervous breakdown and vowed to kill Miss Jones because of his suicidal death. Johnny's mother called the police and tried to get Miss Jones arrested for the murder of her son. The police informed Johnny's mother no charges would be brought against Miss Jones. I will say this in Miss Jones' defense, Johnny had many demons in his life that drove him to that fatal bridge, but I would not have wanted to be the last driver. When people's hearts are tied up in love affairs, that selfish safe man relationship can cut deeply, and someone can be seriously hurt. So, I never want to see a person make a mistake, but I always want to learn from good instruction rather than a dreadful experience. I think enough said on that subject. Miss Jones dated no one for a year after Johnny's death but one day she met Mr. Hammon.

Mr. Hammon left the projects very early every morning about five-thirty am and returned about ten-thirty pm every night. This man was my friend's father, but he kept his addictive habit so well hidden that not one of the neighborhood children knew about his secret. Mrs. Hammon went to work daily. She raised three boys and one daughter in the projects and they never did drugs. Mr. Hammon traveled to Harlem to one hundred sixteenth street, where every morning hundreds of heroin addicts congregated to compile their day's itineraries which consisted of stealing and swindling money from people to make their day's heroine quota. This quota had to be accomplished to avoid violent seizures that would require hospitalization, or you could find yourself involuntarily kicking the habit cold turkey, but this was a dangerous method without medical assistance.

Miss Jones and Mr. Hammon's paths probably would have never crossed but Miss Jones was coming from a neighborhood bar and a dog was lost in the subway tunnel which delayed all trains for two hours. Mr. Hammon was coming out of the subway when Miss Jones was walking by and they started talking and he went to her apartment. Miss Jones had never encountered a man with such a commanding presence. One who spoke with authority and woke up the woman within that Miss Jones never knew existed; it was quite stimulating. Mr. Hammon was the first man Miss Jones felt she could lean on and knew he would not let her fall. Miss Jones was very confused. How can anything be so sweet but at the same time be so terrifying? For the first time in Miss Jones's life, she wasn't playing the man's role in her relationship.

Ever since Miss Jones started wearing that auburn reddish wig, she felt her vagina was superior and held power over any man or any life situation. But now, she found herself waiting by the phone for Mr. Hammons' call and meeting him at the time and the place he said. It was scary.

Now until this time, Miss Jones had only experienced a man that might have drank a little too much, but she had never run into "The Horse" (heroin). Mr. Hammon, of course, had plenty of pipe dreams that he constantly told Miss Jones and because Mr. Hammon was Miss Jones's first love, she believed every word he said. First of all, he promised to get off of heroin and leave his wife of eighteen years. He said they would make a new start in life, but of course, none of this happened. Make no mistake, heroin addiction is a complicated matter with many dimensions that requires your full spiritual and physical cooperation to succeed in kicking the habit. Why Miss Jones thought a roll in the hay was going to stop a heroin habit and make a man leave his wife and children of eighteen years is beyond me. I'll never know what makes a woman think because she does something special for a married man or feels that the sex, she, and another woman's husband has is so exceptional that he will leave his wife. This type of thinking is a grave error. Mr. Hammon must have been tired of his lifestyle with heroin, so he attempted to quit. Something his wife couldn't make him do in eighteen years of marriage. Miss Jones was so happy that her good loving practices had given Mr. Hammon the desire to quit the horse ; she bragged to anyone who would listen. While Mr. Hammon was in the rehab center, Miss Jones, and Mr. Hammon's wife had a nasty argument out of Miss Jones' sixth-floor window in front of all the neighbors. Miss Jones told Mrs. Hammon her husband was going to leave her because "He is deeply in love with me and no longer wants to be married to you!" Mrs. Hammon burst into tears, but she told Miss Jones ``You are nothing more than an outside whore and you will never break up my marriage!"

After three days in rehab, Mr. Hammon came home without completing the detox program. He told Miss Jones she didn't understand, and he ended the relationship that day. Never to revisit it again. I had a few takeaways on the whole situation. First, Mr. Hammon never wanted to be reminded that he tried and failed at drug recovery, and second, every time he looked into Miss Jones's eyes, he saw disappointment. Mr. Hammon's wife accepted him for who he was; a heroin addict, and it was alright with her. Mr. Hammon found the strength to be who he was with his wife and family. Last and most important from the wise words of my mother "It is hard to take a man away from his wife and family." Miss Jones was never the same after her encounter with Mr. Hammon. She stopped dating her neighbor's husbands and decided to go to trade school to become a personal secretary. She got a job with the city and eventually retired. She finally settled down with a White man who was another city worker. She stayed with him for seventeen years until his death.

Miss Eva

(Only Doing What They Understood)

Miss Eva's skin was high yellow, and her hair was past her shoulders. Her hair was a naturally wheat blonde color that matched her skin perfectly. She had deep-set apple green eyes with beautiful thick naturally arched eyebrows. Miss Eva wore about one hundred pounds and stood about five feet two inches tall. Miss Eva had the type of looks that made every woman in the room feel uncomfortable and instantly angry. Miss Eva would have been the perfect arm candy for most men but unfortunately, she had the curse of alcoholism. Therefore, all of her beauty was wasted. She came from a family of alcoholics and only one sister out of eight children escaped this dreadful alcoholic disease. All Miss Eva's brothers remained in the south, but three girls dared to move to New York looking for a better life and Miss Eva was one of them. Miss Eva had two sisters that were equally as beautiful as her. They each had an exotic look different from each other. Their beauty was very much different than the average woman. Some women would become insulted by this statement, but physical attributes are just what they are, physical and some people are just more attractive than others. But what you better know is that your physical attributes have very little to do with your success in life. Being an extremely beautiful woman can be a high jumping point with many advantages in life. But alas, beauty doesn't determine your outcome in life. A beautiful woman, with an empty head that lacks wisdom, is a true formula for a disastrous life; because that same beauty can attract many more men and just people in general who can ruin your life royally if you let them.

Miss Eva lived a life most women in America would have ran away from, but alcoholism, poverty, and lack of self-esteem kept her in a tangled web of being a human doormat. Miss Eva once told my mother that dirt would grow anything. Well in Miss Eva's life it grew everything; everything vile. Such as ignorance, deceitfulness, whorishness, drug addiction, an attitude for accepting life's leftovers, and worst of all, a routine life of hopelessness.

Miss Eva's house and family life reminded me of the color gray. It was like watching a hopeless stray dog aimlessly wandering around on a dirty snowy street, with only its life left to lose. Her living room couches were very old, and they seemed to tell a story about their past; about the amount of abuse they had suffered and witnessed. What I can say, is that this furniture had the same step and temperament of Miss Eva and her hopeless family. You would be hard-pressed to even believe this furniture had ever been brand new. They say Miss Eva was being let out of a friend's car when she saw the furniture sitting on the sidewalk waiting for the garbage truck. Sadly, it had gotten wet because it had been drizzling on and off all day. It might have been better for the furniture if it had been in a hard downpour because it might have washed away some of the mildew and dinginess. It was a horrid piece of furniture. Even though this furniture was wet and carrying the smell of other people's moldy odors and old farts, it was better than going back to her apartment that had absolutely no furniture other than the old cot her husband slept on at night. Miss Eva ran to her apartment building to get her family members to help but as luck would have it, the neighborhood boys were standing around waiting for the rain to slack before they could get on with their football game. During this era, children respected their elders, so the boys gladly agreed to help Miss Eva carry the furniture to her apartment. However, the rain had made the dirt in the couches quite sticky, much like paste, and no one wanted to touch them. Miss Eva saw the boy's initial disdain for her most treasured living room set that God had allowed her to find. So, Miss Eva made a joke about being blessed and how she had such handsome and strong boys to help her move furniture into her apartment. Well apparently, stroking their egos did the trick because they manned up and brought this vile smelly furniture into her apartment. It was a complete living room set, but at the end of each couch arm, the fabric had worn so thin the dirty cotton padding was exposed. Miss Eva saw nothing unbecoming about her new furniture. She was so excited to finally have living room furniture inside her home and she wanted everybody in the family to join in with an appreciative attitude. Originally, the couches must have been a light blue, grey, and black tweed. But over years, all of the threads in the fabric had fused together and became a solid dirty gray. But as months turned into years the furniture started to fight back viciously in various ways. Whenever the fabric would fray around the arms of the couch the cotton padding would fall out and wood splinters would attack your arms and hands. Spring coils with sharp edges would scrap your legs and draw blood. Due to the amount of alcohol being consumed and spilled on these couches, you would smell like a whiskey barrel if you sat on them. Also, I personally helped Suzanne, Miss Eva's daughter, fight with the couches by sewing up holes and even mending large rips with new material my mother sent to Miss Eva on occasion. Miss Eva and her sisters did their best to wipe down this grimy furniture but after a long and hard battle, everyone in the family had to concede the couch had won. It was a hard task, and I noticed less and less no one was wiping down the sofa.

Miss Eva was married in name only. To say she was the mother of four girls would be a stretch. The girls learned early in life that being a child of an alcoholic mother was truly a struggle. Therefore, they raised themselves, doing the very best they could. Having alcoholic parents causes you to lose your entire childhood. It's an embarrassing and very shameful burden that can take over your entire life. The sense of pride most children have for their parents is taken for granted. Children of alcoholic parents become parents without any authority. They can only make sad appeals to an empty shell that used to house a parent that had left years ago. But as a young child, they continue to beg because they have no one else to turn to.

Miss Eva's husband, Mr. William, physically lived in Miss Eva's apartment but spiritually he was light-years out of her world. Mr. William saw that Miss Eva was a sinking ship and had no ability or desire to float. He decided to abort this ghost ship because the inhabitants had died a long time ago and he would not let it kill him. He never allowed the surrounding waters of that sinking ship to gain any ground on him because he knew it had the lethal ability to be cancer to his wallet and his spirit. Mr. Williams had a cardinal rule to never speak even casually to any woman in our building that did not work outside of her home. It fascinated me how he so blamelessly removed his lifeforce from his wife and children. Most ordinary husbands would have fallen prey to the wretched predicament of their family's suffering. Their whole future would have impeded and come to a grinding halt but not Mr. Williams. This emotionless behavior is in the hearts of most of our male species, but they just don't have the guts to act on it. The only reason I think we don't see more of this type of callousness in men is because the courts have now enforced stronger laws. Women have cunningly learned how not to push the envelope where their husband can notice.

Most women seek help from social services, but Miss Eva's husband had a well-paying job, so he bullied her into not getting help. Every woman knows that sacrifice is not in a man's makeup and only a woman can endure a committed relationship without romantic love. Mr. Williams slept on the couch only during the week Monday through Thursday. His alternative sweet life was spent with his girlfriend every weekend starting on Friday. Mr. Williams's schedule dictated that the family and visitors had to live their lives in shifts according to Mr. Williams' good pleasure. Miss Eva's alcoholic sister and nephews were always visiting during the daytime. Suzanne always invited the girls in the building to play records and dance all day long during the summer. We would practice our dance moves and songs for the talent show. We always won because we were good dancers and we had so much time to develop our talent for the show. We were having fun and it never seemed to bother whoever was passed out on the couch at that time. But at seven-thirty pm all socializing came to an abrupt halt. Mr. Williams's sleeping chamber was the living room couch, and it was centrally located in the apartment by the kitchen. The front door was also off-limits because you could not avoid passing his sleeping chamber to get to a bedroom or to return to the front of the house. Therefore, at seven-thirty pm we left no questions asked. The whole building knew Miss Eva's predicament, so the neighbors abided by this rule of no noise in or close to Mr. Williams's sleeping chamber. You would have never thought such a strict no trespassing and no noise policy could have been enforced in a family that had such small children, Miss Eva's burdensome family of drunks that visited daily, and a crowd of inconsiderate teenagers for neighbors. But apparently, Mr. Williams spoke softly but carried a big stick because there he slept every night of the week Mr. Williams taught those dropouts from society one sure thing, he who pays the cost is truly the boss. I've only heard about one violation of the no trespassing decree that occurred. It involved a breach of the couch. During Mr. Williams, hours of slumber some unfortunate soul dared to defy his orders of absolute quiet and no trespassing in his sleeping chamber. Miss

Jones told me that without saying a word Mr. Williams leaped up, grabbed Miss Eva, and pulled her hair out by the roots. Needless to say, there was no further conversation in Mr. Williams's sleeping chamber. Mr. Williams left for work at five am every morning and returned about seven forty-five pm every evening eating no meals at home.

Mr. Williams somewhat knew his two oldest daughters Suzanne and Betty because they came a long way before his final spiritual departure from his family. Long before I made their acquaintance, Miss Eva had become like vinegar to Mr. Williams' teeth. But I am quite sure every time Mr. Williams thought about that year-old baby, and how he had allowed himself to go into that drunk woman's bed that last time. I know Mr. Williams chastised his flesh royally for having led him astray once again. Miss Eva was not innocent in the matter because she was allowing her brother-law to know her biblically way for a lousy fifteen dollars a week so who knew if that last baby was Mr. Williams. But because he had tapped it once without a raincoat, Mr. Williams couldn't disprove the child without a lot of red tape that he was just not prepared to deal with; so, he let it rest. But I can tell you this with certainty, Mr. Williams's dedication was only to his goals. He absolutely positively did not give a flying rat's tail about any of those children's genealogy. Mr.

Williams's only ambition was to live as cheaply as he could and to have as little interaction with his family as humanly possible.

When Mr. Williams spoke to anyone in that apartment it was to tell them to shut the hell up and stay out of the living room while he was trying to get some sleep. Every Thursday Mr. Williams brought home two brown bags containing some of the lowest caliber food that could be bought for ten dollars per week. The two bags usually contained one pound of lard, five pounds of white dirt potatoes, one dozen small eggs, two pounds of neck bones, two pounds of chicken necks, one loaf of day-old bread, two pounds of crack rice, two large cans of pork and beans, and two pounds of the cheapest, sickest hot dogs that could legally be called food. Miss Eva had to borrow any other embellishments such as salt and pepper from neighbors. Mr. Williams wanted no trouble with social services and where else could he live so cheaply for ten dollars per week. Our mothers didn't usually mind giving them all they needed because they realized Miss Eva was in survival mode and thereby the grace of God could be anyone of them.

Miss Eva drank every day, and the children were responsible for getting up and going to school. At the ages of seven, nine, and twelve they went to school because there was nothing else to do and they were assured of breakfast and lunch. When I was about fourteen a severe flu season hit, and it walked through the project like a natural man. I, unfortunately, caught the flu and so did Miss Eva and her two smaller children. My parents had to work so my mother told me to spend the day with the Williams family. My family had lots of over-the-counter cold medicine, so I bought a bag full of it with me, so we could all be as comfortable as possible. My mother had also given me a home remedy medicine and told me to give it to everyone but because it had alcohol in it, I never gave it to Miss Eva because she might have insisted, I take some also. Miss Eva went to her bedroom to take a nap. The children and I were watching TV and all of a sudden Miss Eva came out of her room running towards me screaming with a wild and crazy look. wearing only a filthy raggedy bra and panties. She scared the hell out of me, and the children started screaming and crying. She must have thought about where she could get a drink because she started hollering for Mr. Roberts. Mr. Roberts was a neighbor downstairs who had a thing for her and supplied her drinking habit. I tried to pull Miss Eva from the door. She only weighed about ninety-five pounds, but she flung me away like a rag doll. This really frightened me because I realized I was no match for her desire for a drink. The Williams family didn't have a phone; the children are pulling on me and Miss Eva has now gone down two complete flights of stairs to the third floor. I didn't want to leave the kids by themselves and my mom and Miss Eva's other neighbors on the fifth and six-floor are all at work. I am screaming for Miss Jones, but I knew she took her nerve medicine daily and I would catch hell waking her up. I again hear Miss Eva screaming for Mr. Roberts. Murphy's law is now in full operation because of course Mr. Roberts is not home. But the Lord was with me and Miss Jones heard me yelling so she called 911. I ran downstairs and Mr. Roberts's neighbors have now come out of their homes and they are all trying to help me get her into one of their apartments, but of course, Miss Eva didn't want anything to do with us. Miss Eva is frothing at the mouth; she has the strength of at least two good men and is totally uncooperative. I am still under the foolish delusion that Miss Eva is suffering from a high fever. Miss Jones tells Miss Eva that she has a drink at her house but by this time she is seizing and incoherent and this news is null and void to Miss Eva. Finally, two large police officers arrive and restrain her, and on their heels are the paramedics. I am trying to inform the EMS workers that all Miss Eva's activity has been brought on by a high fever. My story might have had a little more credibility but during the tussle the large bottle of cold remedy my mother had concocted spilled on me, so I smelled like a liquor barrel. To this day I hate the taste and smell of alcohol. If the children and I had known what was truly ailing Miss Eva I would have given her the bottle of medicine and none of this drama would have occurred. They took Miss Eva to the hospital and admitted her to the detox ward, and she dried up for about three days and returned home.

This would have been a golden opportunity for Mr. Williams to eventually move in with his girlfriend but only after she had gotten a good job and all of the children were basically grown. Mr. Williams never divorced Miss Eva. I guess he always felt he would truly outlive an alcoholic. But none of us knows God's plans. Miss Eva lived to enjoy Mr. Williams' social security. But unfortunately, she also outlived her three daughters. Two were taken by the HIV epidemic and the oldest was taken by Hepatitis. Miss Eva had the pleasure of raising all three of her grandchildren.

Miss Lucy

(Only Doing What They Understood)

They tell me when a dog gives birth, even if the puppies look perfectly normal to the human eye, the mother dog can instinctively tell if something is wrong and will immediately eat the defective pups to cut her losses and ensure the survival of her other pups. I am not suggesting Lucy should have been killed at birth. However, an intervention on wisdom should have happened because Lucy was the mother of dumb Dora's. It seems to me that the Bible explains wisdom as close kin to common sense. God tells us wisdom was with him in the beginning and that thoroughly impressed me. A person that lacks common sense is to be grievously pitied because every option in life becomes a pitfall waiting to show the world how they can screw up a free lunch.

To call Lucy a ghetto queen would be insulting to ghetto queens everywhere. A real ghetto queen could train a new person in the department of social services on benefit policies and procedures.

Even ghetto queens in training knew the fatal consequences of allowing their sexual favors to be taken for granted. Your sexual favors had a huge responsibility. It had to produce income those food stamps couldn't reach. Miss Lucy was not a ghetto queen because she had no earthly idea what that vagina she sat upon could accomplish when worked correctly. Men have invaded other countries and sent men to their deaths so that a particular woman could be brought back to them and she would give her sexual pleasures away for a two-liter Pepsi.

I was thirteen when I met Lucy. She was twenty years old and married with three children and one on the way. To say Lucy and her family were poor when they moved into the projects was a true understatement. People moved to the projects for several reasons; seeking a fast track to get on their feet or to escape those hell hole vermin-infested tenement houses that were extremely cold in winter and unbearably hot in summer. Even though the project's architectural design reassembled a huge chicken coop; it was an oasis in the slums. In the projects, you could have all things working for your good. There were all types of amenities; subsidized rent, paid utilities, and if the ghetto powers that be smiled on you that precious money-making body part would connect you with a fine sugar daddy to help you with your other bills.

Well, I must tell you a little about Lucy's history. Her father died early, and her mother Miss Bell was a strict Pentecostal who ruled totally without love or repentance. Threats of hell and damnation were the only way she rolled. Miss Bell and Lucy's aunt had started the wheels turning for Lucy to marry a young and upcoming man in a neighboring church. After meeting him, Lucy felt like she was now condemned to marrying her mother with a penis. Lucy led a sheltered life and she usually attended church three times a week unless there was a revival, and then of course, it was every night. Sadly, Lucy's family attended a church where they were the victims of an evil greedy pastor and his wife. The people of the church were poor with very little education. The pastor taught nothing, not even the word of God. The church policy was floor-length dresses and a prayer cloth on your head at all times. But Lucy's prayer cloth should have been over her vagina because that's what was conjuring up all those sinful thoughts Lucy could not seem to put under subjection.

Lucy was young with no common sense and her adult role models were people of little understanding on how to direct a fourteen-year-old girl. Lucy was built for sports, but her parents said it was sinful for girls to play basketball or any activity that was outside of the church. So, she focused all her attention on physical pleasure and dreamt about her escape from her life of torture. Lucy realized that she had five lovely fingers and a vagina that could make her forget about the frightening life she was going to face with the devil and damnation. Just when Lucy turned fifteen, she figured out those five fingers were nice but there had to be more than this. Lucy needed a connection and a man with sweet words and physical equipment was really what she literally had a burning desire for. Once Lucy met Rick she was hypnotized. She allowed herself to be captured by his worldly ways of living large and by the way he could handle himself in bed. Rick was so much smarter than Lucy in every way. Rick in the famous words of Minister Louis Farrakhan, was a "tragic Mulatto." Rick had a White man's blood in him therefore, he was not afraid to dream way beyond his current living conditions. Rick was jet black with very keen Caucasian features and straight black hair. You could say that he was handsome in an odd sort of way because he had an Australian look. Rick had the good fortune to travel with his mother and her rich White employer to different parts of the world. Rick constantly bragged about his White heritage. I found him to be obnoxious and when he got on my nerves with that train of thought I showed him my cup of care which was empty. Rick was raised by a single mother who had an important position as the head housekeeper for some very rich White people. His mother Isabel thought it was crucial for children to be exposed to the better things of life and was determined to give Rick a large piece of the American pie. As Yogi would say, Rick was smarter than the average bear because back in the day this Negro graduated at seventeen from Catholic high school with honors. With help from his mother's employers, he got accepted to Columbia University.

In Rick's first year of college, there was a terrible turn of events. He met long leg Lucy and it was downhill from that moment on. Nobody could persuade him that Lucy was not marriage material and that he should have banged it and moved on or lease paid more attention to birth control. What all of those who were not in bed with Lucy soon found out to their hurt was that twelve years of Catholic school had a strong effect on Rick to do the right thing. The only thing that Lucy brought to the table was an extremely tight snatching vagina that Rick simply could not get enough of. Lucy's marriage to Rick overwhelmed his mother. It left her exhausted and in a broken state of affairs. All of Isabel's sacrifices and dreams for her son to attend law school slowly drizzled down the tubes with each consecutive baby Lucy continued to spit out. Lucy adapted to that birthing table as if she had invented it. I think she would have had Lucy killed if she had the nerve to ask one of those rich White employers for the money to make the arrangements and a second mortgage on her home was out of the question for the simple fact she still had to educate Rick's younger sister.

Lucy's mother knew from the start that Rick was sent from the very pits of hell to ruin her family. Lucy was pregnant within a month after meeting Rick. Lucy's mother immediately felt her daughter's soul was lost forever seeing how her Christianity was not big on repenting and forgiveness. Lucy was made to leave her mother's house and had to live with Rick's family. Lucy's mother totally abandoned her because she was disgusted and could no longer stand the sight of her daughter. Living with Rick's mother Isabel was a dark time for Lucy because Isabel hated her and made no secret of how she blamed Lucy for her son's failure. Rick had quite a few get rich schemes that actually seemed on the surface doable. Isabel still believed in her son's potential and poured large amounts of money into Rick's ventures, but none worked out in his favor. Rick was a book smart person and had grown accustomed to having his way for many years. Now even the least bit of constructive criticism sent him into a ghetto "I know it all, tell me nothing" attitude. This attitude Rick had developed over the years was only for the very rich and accomplished, not for someone looking for a break in life. Isabel became convinced it was a dumb spiritual curse that came with Lucy and it had now connected itself to her son. Rick was already a husky-built person so when he started consoling himself with food after each failure, he quickly grew to four hundred and fifty funky pounds. Rarely does an upcoming fat man have a chance for an executive training position. It is most difficult to be charming at four fifty hundred and darn near impossible to raise any good times in bed. Lucy was in the situation room with three children, no money, no education, a four hundred and fifty pounds know it all man and the worse thing was she had no common sense. The last straw came when Rick stole three thousand dollars from his mom to start a drum and bugle corps. He had convinced himself that taking them on tour would generate a fortune. Get rich schemes are for TV and that's where Rick should have left those highfalutin get rich ideas, in TV land. Isabel told them to move immediately, and of course, they couldn't go to Lucy's mother's house so off to the shelter they went. They were people cut off from family and friends, but Lucy met a real ghetto queen at the shelter with the knowledge to help them maneuver through the policies, procedures, and the benefits of the Welfare System. Which in turn, got them out of their terrible web of poverty. They were most fortunate to get a kind social worker that got them a quick apartment in the projects which Rick hated. He felt he was way above the people that lived in the projects but being cut off from his mother purse string for the first time he now had the choices of beggars and we know all their options are few.

For Lucy to finally be on her own this apartment in the projects was definitely a power move for Lucy. She would be in charge for eight fabulous hours while Rick was at work. So, without further ado, Lucy was on the prowl for even more capable partners. It became crystal clear these partners came only with sex on their minds and the only thing that they might provide is one liquid protein meal to Lucy at a time. Lucy met a city worker who was built right and had plenty of action. He became Lucy's regular guy. His name was Larry. He was a real frequent flyer, visiting once or twice a week and sometimes three when his work schedule permitted. Even at my young age and you have got to remember I knew every. I thought this was a bit risky but then again the sex they were enjoying was not rocking my boat, so what did I care. He worked for the city as a dog catcher. Is that ironic or what. I don't know if the lovemaking had him love crazy or was it just the thrill of having sex with another man's wife in that man's bed. Lucy was like a farm girl who now has seen the bright lights of ***Sex in The City*** and she was not about to return to those five fingers. Lucy felt since the children were young and unable to express themselves fully, she didn't have to be careful about what they saw. Her daughter Cheryl unfortunately was more articulate than Lucy imagined. To Lucy's surprise Rick asked each child who had been to visit that day the two younger children managed to let him know that Big

Bird had made an appearance and the shocker was Cheryl told him every neighbor that darted Lucy's door. Thank God for Lucy none of her gentlemen callers had come that day. Lucy locked the children in their rooms regularly because she knew Rick would have whipped her behind unmercifully or worse yet put the entire family on welfare and be home every day.

I had not noticed Larry's dog truck parked right in front of the entrance of the projects. It was a hot summer day so there were about twenty people out on the bench laughing, drinking beer and some were even smoking marijuana. It was a great day, and I wasn't paying attention and didn't see Rick going into our building. All of sudden we see Larry jump out of Lucy's third-floor window. I guess Larry wasn't a fast thinker because jumping out of a third-floor window would not have been my very first thought. We can all agree he was not the sharpest knife in the drawer. There are very few places to hide in a small apartment for a guilty back doorman. When Larry jumped out the window he must have tried to land on his feet and he did, but the human body's legs don't have shock absorbers, so he rolled on to his back. He jumped straight up but he was in a daze and started to hobble around in a circle because that third-floor jump was no joke. He had broken his ankle. What amazed me was that he only broke his ankle. Larry landed in the grass which was enclosed by a five-foot fence. Larry looked simply pitiful struggling to climb that fence in a hurry with a broken ankle. Larry later told me he was concerned Rick had heard him go out the window and he knew with a broken ankle he was no match for a viciously angry husband. The boys that were out there said Larry needed no help because superman could handle a mere third-floor jump. People were laughing so much they couldn't pull themselves together to give Larry a hand over the fence and out of the grass. He finally got someone to give him a hand over the fence and hobbled to his ASPC truck. By that evening the entire project was talking and laughing about Larry's spectacular superman heroic jump. We all loved and enjoyed it to the max.

The next day I was extremely anxious to speak to Lucy to get the most intimate details that led up to Larry having to jump out of her third-floor apartment window. The very first thing I wanted to know was, what was she and Larry doing when Rick came to the door? Lucy said they were on the floor going at like animals and she heard Rick put the key in the door. Well, Lucy can believe that if she likes but she was not living in a rundown clapboard house but in the projects where the walls are fortified and pretty soundproof. Lucy would have to have the sonar senses of a dolphin to have heard that key enter that lock three and a half rooms away. I believe Rick had a suspicion that perhaps that dumb Dora of a wife actually had a man in that single twin bed that they so uncomfortably shared. Rick had many things to consider at that door. Weighing four hundred and fifty pounds limits the places you could readily lay your head and because of past misdeeds, his family was not an option. Poor people don't have clubs or usually have available money for a hotel room and if you were to lose your spot without notice who is going to shelter you. If by chance someone had an extra bargain-basement bed, they were not going to allow your big funky behind to tear it up and of course, a fold-out cot would be out of the question. I cannot imagine the amount of nerve it would take to ask someone if I weighed four hundred and fifty pounds to allow me to totally destroy their living room couch. A normal young man's sexual appetite is red hot and Rick's conversation revealed that sex truly consumes ninety-nine and a half percent of his thoughts in life. I am quite sure at four hundred plus pounds Rick was paranoid that each lay he got would be his very last. The one thing we all know is that sex cost money whether you buy it outright or it is cunningly taken away from a man by a skilled wife. If a man is to maintain a continual flow of these niceties from any woman money must be spent. Rick had a minimum wage job as a security guard at a low-end department store which was very shaky because he was stealing and selling dresses undercover. His wife got a small check from welfare that kept the family barely afloat. Weighing four hundred pounds and without the necessary money for a new woman, if things went sideways with his current woman a blow-up doll seemed to making her appearance in the wings. So, there were some really tough decisions to be made at that moment and because Rick did not know what to do, Being a huge 450 pounds with no money he had nowhere to go so he decided to just make some noise. Maybe if a man was in the house they would figure out something and hide in a closet until he went in the back bedroom.

Rick was now seeing the real Lucy. But it was a lot too late, a matter of fact it was a lot too late three kids ago. Every time Rick thought about all the missed opportunities he allowed to slip away because he could not control his sexual appetite it gave him nightmares. Rick never lost all his anxiety and his dream of becoming a lawyer dissolved like the dewdrops in the noonday sun. And my dear Lucy, well she continued to be that housewife without any real ambition for anything more than a roll in the hay and a two-liter Pepsi. May God be with any new man that Lucy encounters.

Miss Barbara

(Old women stupid mistakes)

We never want to make mistakes and having a kind heart or just seeking a clear conscience. our desire is that no one else makes mistakes. I pray that good instructions will always be my take away rather than my having to endure horrible experiences. Two women making bad choices late in life suffered because they did not know their worth. Sadly their life of misery persisted due to their inability to hear God a voice of sound instruction so as to correct the woeful situations quickly.

Miss Barbara was a sweet person and as the saying goes, she would not hurt a fly. She was an attractive woman, with big beautiful legs that she always made sure they were on display 24/7. Miss Barbara had a sweet motherly smile that made men and women trust her with some of their most intimate secrets. This inviting smile would prove to be a very helpful trait in her new and upcoming sex trade business. You could say that she was a full-figured woman without being fat. Miss Barbara had a nondescript face that would **easily** blend into a pride of lions on the wide-open spaces of the Serengeti. Her hair was thick and curly; she always framed her face so that it resembled a lion's mane. Miss Barbara's complexion was a dirty blondish brown and there were freckles on her face. Therefore she really did remind me of a lioness and she would prove to have all the stealthy traits of a good lioness. Miss Barbara was the first black person I had ever known to have freckles but somehow they made her look attractive. Miss Barbara wore everything khaki; her favorite colors were tan and muted green. All of Miss Barbara's clothes had a square cut so it always looked as if she were wearing a tent which would have been very much appropriate for the wild tall grasses of the Serengeti. But for my living in color diva taste, I found all those muted earth tones to be a waste of good material.

Miss Barbara dyed her hair light brown to match her complexion but more importantly, this color also helped to explain why her oldest child had natural auburn hair. I was told that Miss Barbara suffered a divorce from an exceptionally good man due to an irresponsible lustful affair with a womanizer. After losing her husband she was forced to move into the project. Mr. Ray moved into the project with Miss Barbara; he was a lazy loser that now had carte blanche with all the lonely single women. He would not work in a pie factory and tried his hand at running numbers but his doggishness soon got him into trouble. Once he started sleeping with these women they no longer wanted to pay for their numbers and those that had husbands barred him from their homes. After months of this type going on, Miss Barbara s decided that this no good Negro could give two cents about her or that little red-haired girl. Never to be blessed with another good man Miss Barbara struck out three more times and gained three more baby daddies just say not judging.

Miss Barbara carried herself as a hard-working sophisticated lady. Due to a serious heart condition, Miss Barbara was unable to work a full-time job. Because I was attending to my Motown life in the project and keeping my crown straight during my many activities left little time to fully investigate Miss Barbara's illness. But I knew her situation was dire because I heard she had only one hearing at the board of disability without the benefit of a lawyer. The word in the project was she had grabbed the gold ring and was "awarded the full compensation disability package." They say the clerk of courts informed the judge of Miss Barbara's diagnosis he hit the gavel once Miss Barbara's full package was now law of land. You know how people carry on they said she jumped like James Brown and said "I feel good like I knew that I would." Because Miss Barbara's work history was quite impressive it dated back to her early teens therefore her disability check was nice!!! Everyone has had a day to see the Money Lamp but that day Miss Barbara got to see it shine. That very same day Family Court also awarded her child support from all those children's fathers that could be located. Miss Barbara, being a very enterprising, lioness had quite a few covert activities going on under those mild muted tents that she used as everyday camouflage. Miss Barbara was very discreet but operated a top-dollar bootlegging business that encompassed two different projects. Her hours of operation were Sundays and of course all those hours that the liquor store was closed. Since Miss Barbara had three boys and a girl, the project's very strict guidelines concerning the number of rooms a tenant is entitled to rent; Miss Barbara qualified for a three bedroom apartment. For her most cautious and closest friends, a bedroom was designed for those in need of a special getaway. A particular project architectural design built for fire safety turned out to be the greatest feature of Miss Barbara's quickie den. Three adjoining buildings with a flat roof and high borders made escaping to any of the other buildings child's play. Women were able to meet men at Miss Barbara under the cloak of buying liquor or visiting anyone of the many women that lived in the three adjoining buildings. Those who had many eyes watching them could enter any of the three buildings across the roof and go right into Miss Barbara's sixth-floor apartment. This bedroom was designed to accommodate those that desired a lustful encounter but had to be completely incognito in the wee hours of the night or during school time. Only a very few knew about her sex trade business but as always sex yields a large profit. So, you see Miss Barbara's little hideaway was the cheater's oasis.

Miss Barbara was stealthy as those big cats she resembled but when it came to her relationship with men she was sad and was self-loathing. As you know I had made it my life's assignment to gather grown folks' information. But my Project's life agenda consumes so much of my valuable time that the plotting and planning that is required to get accurate adult gossip had to be put on the back burner. As I chronologically grew, I now provided my mother with great amusement with my analytical review of her girlfriend's situation, therefore she enthusiastically brought me all her juicy tidbits. As the story goes Mr. Billy was Miss Barbara's boyfriend for over ten years. Over forty years Mr. Billy owned a pool hall that was a few doors down from the liquor store that was located across the street from the project. If location means anything in business Mr. Billy had all bases covered. He was about ten years older than Miss Barbara with grown children and no mortgage and wife he kept tuck away on Long Island. All things were working for him because any time he wanted to stay the night with Miss Barbara simply told his wife he was too tired to drive to the island. Mr. Billy's abusive relationship with Miss Barbara started way before our family moved into the project and ended when Miss Barbara passed away. To keep the fighting and the verbal abuse down to a minimal level Miss Barbara was extremely careful to avoid stirring up Mr. Billy's anger triggers.

My mother sent me to Miss Barbara's house to pick up tickets for an event that Mr. Billy and Miss Barbara were sponsoring that evening. Here again, a dog comes into play and as always it ends in a mess. He was a huge beautiful all-white German shepherd that behaved perfectly well in Miss Barbara's presence. She went into the bedroom to retrieve the tickets and that is when the trouble started. The dog walked slowly over to me. I didn't want any excitement, so I backed up against the wall. I was so fearful that the saliva in my mouth instantly dried up leaving me speechless and faint. Because I was so frightened my knees buckled and I went down on the floor. He quickly advanced, placing his front paws on my shoulders and his back paws at the sides of my hips. Miss Barbara's house was also decorated in that elaborate Louis the 16th style just like my mother and Miss Rudy's. Her drapes went across the entire living room wall. Since my back was against the wall when I went down to the floor all the drapes came down too. Because that horrible animal had a supersonic hearing, he heard Mr. Billy come off the elevator and quickly jumped, off of me and went happily to the door to greet his master. Mr. Billy walked in at that moment and demanded to know why his very expensive drapes were on the floor. There was way more trouble in store for me and poor Miss Barbara because Mr. Billy was furious!!! I instantly assessed the situation, which was dire. I don't know if Miss Barbara was more afraid or embarrassed by the verbal abuse or horrible beating she knew would follow. The dog started to growl at Mr. Billy, and he quickly changed his tone and escorted the dog to the bedroom. Right then I knew he probably always locked the dog away first whenever he was going to beat poor Miss Barbara up. The lull in the conversation presented a prime opportunity for me to immediately start an explanation about what had happened. He was still not completely satisfied because he then started to chastise Miss Barbara for leaving me along with the dog. I appealed to his ego and told him how much I loved his big beautiful dog and what a good job he had done with training such a big fierce animal. I informed him that I begged Miss Barbara to play with the dog and that is how drapes came down. Being such an egotistical creep he ate it up like candy and offered to take care of putting back the drapes. I stayed and helped Mr. Billy and we all enjoyed a pleasant time with the dog. When I got home I reenacted the entire episode for mother and sister. My mother was ever so grateful that I had saved Miss Barbara from a terrible beating episode my sister and I agreed that Mr. Billy should have been carted off to jail.

I also let my Mom know that pitiful Miss Gloria had come by to get her tickets even though this night would not be the glorious night it would have been just seven short months ago. The story was that Miss Gloria was only married for seven months but unfortunately, Miss Gloria's state of bliss would be very short-lived. Miss Gloria, just like all the other single women in the project, was continuously in search of the man that would procure them that white picket fence. Miss Gloria was a few years younger than my mother's crowd. Miss Gloria was probably even more concerned than the other older women because she saw firsthand how you can end up living in this rock n roll barrel of crabs for eternity with no companion. It was truly a bleak future therefore time was of the essence because she was at the age that tomorrow she could be middle age. Right now Miss Gloria looked a lot younger than her age and was able to maintain a youthful size fourteen. Miss Gloria was high yellow with long thick nappy hair that she kept under excellent control with a very hot comb and the Lord knows she knew how to make that comb do what it does. She was a very attractive woman who had a good sense of fashion. Having three girls Miss Gloria found it most advantageous to work at a sewing factory so her skills were second to none on the machine. Because She had all these things going for her and being single flirtation was her downfall.

My mother told me that Miss Gloria had an annoying habit that once she became intoxicated; her dress would always accidentally fly up real high in your man's face. From my mom's vivid description there was quite a bit of rump to see and it also did a little surprise shimmy whenever it made an appearance. My mother told my father "I will put your eyes out the next time I see your eyes glued to Miss Gloria's talented rump. Miss Gloria's behind was a hot topic amongst the women. It wasn't the biggest it just seemed to have the most tricks up its sleeve if you get what I mean. Miss Jones had promised the ladies the next time that rump was in her man's face she was going to give it a good swift kick.

Miss Gloria had followed the same non producing regimes for getting a man as other women who have gone before her. Wishing and hoping and thinking and plotting and planning and going to clubs meeting one married man after another never getting any fulfillment in your life. Most times when you do it your way it eventually goes south because God was not in it, to begin with. A very wise woman told me to stay before the Lord and if there is a chance that will be the one.

Miss Gloria was a good mother that loved her children and did what she understood to ensure their life was better than hers had been. All of her four children were for the same stupid ex-husband that she had the good sense to divorce. She had gotten pregnant for Mr. Melvin and as you know back in the day the shotgun was always ready to make its' appearance any time the rag was not red and those old ladies checked monthly. Mr. Melvin was a real jerk, a momma's boy, a runaround, an explosive temper, and he would break everything in the house when angry. I not talking about breaking a few dishes this Negro here would destroy the furniture chop any soft cushion or mattress into bits and throw anything that would fit in the incinerator shoot. So you literally had nothing left in your apartment because when left for a day or so he would throw away all of their clothes. Unfortunately, Miss Glory's oldest daughter Lena inherited her father's traits that plagued the child from birth to high school graduation. Procreating with idiots will only produce the same tendencies in your children. Motown went all the way to California and brought us Brenda Holloway to let us know that Every Little Bit Hurts so they did mention men like him. I guess we were not listening.

Miss Gloria finally met a man Mr.Troy that had the power and the desire to take her away from the project. All ladies were buzzing with excitement because he was the real thing, single, hardworking, and appeared to be true blue. Lena was now nineteen with a strong desire to be an actress and would work anywhere other than the performing arts. Miss Gloria could not afford to pay for Lena's acting lessons without help from her by getting at least a part-time job. After Miss Gloria and Mr. Troy got married it became worse and Lena became more disrespectful to Mr. Troy. Lena overheard Mr. Troy say that if she wanted to be an actress then she had better help with her school. Lena developed deep vengeful hate for Mr. Troy and once she heard that he was moving her mother to Long Island. Lena told her family she was getting into character and started only wearing bathing suits around the apartment in the dead of winter. Miss Gloria told my mother "that one night Lena was going into the bathroom and Mr. Troy said he grabbed her breast so she broke a bottle and came after him." Mr. Troy denied and said, "that Lena was crazy like her father and that he was not going to live under those conditions."

Mr. Troy demanded that Miss Gloria move with him immediately to his brother's house with the other children. Miss Gloria said that she would stay in the project until the sale of the house closed. But Mr. Troy refused to allow Lena to dart at his door. Can you blame him? Lena was already missing quite a few cards in her deck and once she started to drink heavily she became an absolute fool. Lena's father was a great role model for how to destroy family life. Lena really started acting out because she could see that her mother was considering leaving with Mr. Troy. Miss Gloria was in turmoil but after a while, peer pressure from those women who had no man or even the possibility of getting one. Miss Gloria decided to let Lena stay and told Mr. Troy that she would join him later. Well that idea went right down the toilet. My mother said she would have never taken Lena anywhere or even allowed her to follow in her new life. Well, once Lena had gotten rid of her Mother's husband and felt secure that she had broken up her mother's marriage within about six months she hooked up with some man and went to the Virgin Island to make movies never to live with Miss Gloria again. Miss Gloria never got an opportunity to move out of the project and Mr. Troy never trusted Miss Gloria again and their relationship dwindled. The Lord said that we have the responsibility of raising our children but they are only a loan because mates are for a lifetime to enjoy.

Most of the women were sad for Miss Gloria and I know some were beating the Tambourines rejoicing at her demise. Miss Barbara I believe was sincerely grieved over how things turned out for Miss Gloria but the Blind can not lead the blind because truly Miss Barbara had some real troubles brewing herself

Miss Barbara's four children endured their mother being mentally and physically abused by Mr. Billy for many years. Miss Barbara and Mr. Billy both had a piss, poor excuse for their abusive relationship. She actually blamed herself, because she was heard to say many times, he only hits me when he is drinking, which a horrible excuse for being someone's punching bag. I overheard my mother and Miss Rudy discussing how Miss Barbara was always walking on eggshells whenever she spoke around Mr. Billy because she had to be most cautious not to arouse his anger. After being totally grossed out by Mr. Billy my mother said that Mr. Billy publicly spoke about Miss Barbara's bazaar sexual appetites in mixed company and before her children, now he truly was nothing. His mode of operation was to beat Miss Barbara late at night usually leaving no scars but neighbors could hear her begging for mercy and they would call the cops, but she would never press charges. Several times when he lost total control and blackened Miss Barbara's eye or boxed her face until she looked awful. Men have been known to approach Mr. Billy at the pool hall about hitting such a refine woman as Miss Barbara. He always replied that he had a terrible temper and it would sometimes get the best of him. He always assured them he was really working on controlling his emotions, but she always pushed him way too far. But alas he was working on it so all was well and it probably would not happen again. And we all know that pigs do fly.

Miss Barbara's middle boy Donald must have been sired by a Ken Norton type because this boy was built as if he had been pressed weights every day. At fifteen this boy stood at 6feet one inch tall and his weight was about 200 muscle-bound pounds. I don't know if this had anything to do with the boy's physique, but he started losing his hair at the early age of fifteen. Miss Barbara finally told my mother that Donald's father was a real live sugar daddy that was 32 years her senior. Therefore, Donald aged as if he were twenty-five, yet he was only fifteen. Mr. Billy must have thought about how fast Donald was maturing and the absolute muscle mass this boy's body had developed in such a short time. It was as if God himself had raised this boy up just to help Mr. Billy with his unmanageable temper. My mother and I decided that Mr. Billy was afraid of Donald because he had stopped hitting Miss Barbara whenever the boys were around and if did hit her, he kept it under control so that it was undetectable.

I can remember it clearly it was a Jewish high holy day, so schools were closed but Mr. Billy was unaware of this fact. He had not beaten Miss Barbara in quite some time so this was an ideal time for him to lose his temper while the boys were at school, but this would prove to be a grave error because he was dead wrong. I heard Donald explaining the events to the policemen that led up to him hospitalizing Mr. Billy. He said that "Mr. Billy came into the house violently cussing Miss Barbara and accusing her for having just put some man out of his bed which was an outright lie." Donald said, "Mr. Billy slapped Miss Barbara so hard that it knocked her to the floor, but this time I stepped in and Mr. Billy was the next person to hit the floor." Donald was beating Mr. Billy with nine years of rage that came from having to hear his mother cry and beg for mercy and he was unable to defend her. I had the whole incident from good authority that Donald beat Mr. Billy out of the apartment and threw him down those hard cement steps hitting that iron railing as he went down. But was not finished on the fifth floor he busted up Mr. Billy's face and threw down the next flight of stairs. Mr. Billy realized that he was no match for this monster boy so he tried to get away by running and screaming for help but no one dared to interfere the boy was frosting at the mouth. It was reported that on the fourth floor, Donald was beating Mr. Billy as if he had just gotten started. It was terrible, this boy was wearing Mr. Billy's behind out. He threw down to the third floor now Mr. Billy was just a rag doll there was no more fight in him he was for all intent and purpose an unconscious man. Miss Barbara was the only one able to approach Donald at this point because he was still so angry. I heard that she really had to beg and use all her skills as his mother to convince him not to finish killing Mr. Billy. By this time the police had arrived they were familiar with what went on at this address, but this time it had a different outcome because Mr. Billy left in the ambulance. The policemen took Donald's statement and left. I understand Mr. Billy had two broken bones in his face, three broken ribs, one broken leg, a collapsed lung and cuts and bruises that required too many stitches to mention. Let the record be crystal clear this could not have happened to a better person. Mr. Billy never had a temper problem again in life with Miss Barbara or anyone else that I ever heard of. Mr. Billy wanted nothing to do with pressing charges because he would then have had to tell his wife that his girlfriend's son beat him to a pulp. Mr. Billy told his wife that he had been a victim of a brutal smuggling. Mr. Billy's predicament of not being able to press charges against Donald presented an ideal opportunity for the police. The officers made Miss Barbara an offer she could not refuse. Law enforcement would not persue any charges against Donald if Miss Barbara gave up her all her illegal activites. Miss Barbara reluctantly agreed to the officers terms to save Donald from doing time. Long after this happened, anytime that someone in the project got beat up they would refer back to and compare whether the beating was in the same caliber of Mr. Billy's behind whooping.

The Bible said that man is grass and life is as fragile as a vapor. Then why would anyone allow themselves to be beaten and live a life of shame for so many years that you had the power to walk away? Miss Barbara was not a young impressionable girl when she met Mr. Billy. Loneliness and being afraid that you will never find anyone else can make a woman snatch at very small crumbs of happiness that bring such, long cycles of misery. I think about how Miss Barbara allowed 17 years of her life to be spent blaming herself for Mr. Billy's cruel and abusive behavior.

I pray that you and I will always have Godly wisdom so that you nor I will be an old woman making stupid mistakes.

Appreciation

I trust that you have enjoyed reading this book as much as I have enjoyed writing it!. Please leave a 5 – Star review for me on Amazon, along with your honest feedback.

Thank You!

About The Author

The author Savannah Kennedy was born in South Carolina and moved to Brooklyn as a young child. She grew up in the infamous Macy projects – where rapper and business mogul Shawn Carter aka Jay – Z was raised. Her strong goals and the need to help others always guided her decisions as she embarked upon careers in the teaching, medical, and insurance industry. She is an active member of her church and currently resides in South Carolina with her husband and their fur babies – 1 cat and 1 dog.

Savannah is a woman who trusts and loves God and always seeks His wisdom in every life situation. She acknowledges that she is a gifted and anointed woman whose life has fostered many lessons to share with the world – writing this book is one such way.

She strives to speak into the lives of other women, in hopes that they will avoid some of the pain and disappointments that she herself has experienced. Her urgent message to mothers is: "Be a shining example to your children, especially your daughters and teach them well. Give them a head start on understanding life and how to navigate it in a productive and meaningful manner."

Made in the USA
Middletown, DE
22 August 2021

46651016R00121